Kristy's Book

Kristy's Book

Ann M. Martin

AN
APPLE
PAPERBACK

SCHOLASTIC INC.
New York Toronto London Auckland Sydney

The author gratefully acknowledges
Jeanne Betancourt
for her help in
preparing this manuscript.

Major League Baseball trademarks and
copyrights used with permission of Major
League Baseball Properties Inc.

Cover photograph copyright © Gary Randall/FSG Intl.

Interior art and cover drawing by Angelo Tillery

Cover painting by Hodges Soileau

ISBN 0-590-69181-3

12 11 10 9 8 7 6 5 4 3 2 1   6 7 8 9/9 0 1/0

Printed in the U.S.A.   40

First Scholastic printing, September 1996

CHAPTER 1

It was ten o'clock on a sunny Saturday morning. Normally, I play softball, baby-sit, or hang out with my friends on Saturday mornings. But I had a big English project due Monday. All the eighth-graders at my school (Stoneybrook Middle School) have to write autobiographies. So there I was, inside the house on a beautiful day, writing the story of my life from the time I was born until the present. If I was going to hand in the fascinating story of my life on time, I had to work on it all weekend. I felt grumpy as I sat at my desk and opened my notebook.

Suddenly my bedroom door flew open and my seven-year-old stepsister, Karen, ran in. "Karen," I said, "you're supposed to knock, remember?"

Karen shushed me with a finger to her lips, sprawled herself on the floor, and wriggled under my bed.

Before I could wonder what she was up to, Andrew burst into my room. Andrew is Karen's four-year-old brother and my stepbrother. A blue bath towel was tied around his neck like a cape and a pink Halloween mask covered the upper half of his face.

"What's going on, Batman?" I asked.

"I have to catch the Joker!" Andrew shouted, opening my closet door and looking in.

Then my mother walked into my room asking, "Kristy, honey, have you seen Sam?" Sam's my fifteen-year-old brother.

"Sam took David Michael to softball practice," I replied. David Michael is my seven-year-old brother. He plays on my softball team, Kristy's Krushers. I organized the team for kids who aren't ready for Little League.

"Why didn't *you* take him?" she asked. "Aren't you going to the Krushers' practice?"

"I can't. I have to work on my English project," I explained.

Mom sat on my bed. "I was going to ask Sam to watch the younger kids while Nannie and I make a hospital visit to Mrs. Randal."

"Where's Karen?" Bath-towel Batman demanded of my mother. "She's the Joker. I have to catch her."

"I don't know, Andrew," my mother answered. "But if she's the Joker she's probably hiding from you."

Just then Nannie, my grandmother, waltzed into my room with Emily. Emily is my two-and-a-half-year-old adopted sister. Shannon, David Michael's puppy, followed them in and plopped down at my feet. My room was becoming Grand Central Station.

Nannie sat on my bed next to my mother. Emily stood in the middle of my room, looking around. I could tell she was thinking, "Now what can I play with in here?"

I folded a piece of note paper into an airplane and flew it in her direction. "Here, Emily," I said. "Airplane."

"Could you baby-sit, Kristy?" my mother asked.

"Mom, I told you I have to — " I was interrupted by Charlie, my oldest brother, who's seventeen. "Kristy, do you have my Stoneybrook High jacket?"

"I saw it in the backseat of your car yesterday," I told him.

"Thanks," he said. "It must still be there."

He sat on my desk — on top of my notebook. "What's going on in here?" he asked.

"I was trying to do my homework," I answered.

"And I'm trying to figure out what to do

with the younger children while Nannie and I are out for an hour or so," my mother added. "Could you watch them, Charlie? We'll be back by lunchtime."

Charlie picked up a Spalding ball from my desk and rolled it to Emily. She giggled as she ran for it. "I have an out-of-town football game today," Charlie said.

Emily held out the ball to Andrew. "Ball," she informed him.

Bath-towel Batman sat on the floor. Emily plopped down facing him and they started rolling the ball back and forth.

"What about Watson?" I asked. Watson is my stepfather. Karen and Andrew are his kids from his first marriage.

"Watson's running errands this morning," Nannie explained. "He's already left."

"What about you, Kristy?" my mother asked. "Can you sit?"

"Mo-om!" I moaned. I pointed to the pile of papers and photographs on my desk. "My autobiography?"

"Sorry," she said. "I forgot."

"Why didn't you call the Baby-sitters Club during our meeting yesterday?" I asked. "Then you wouldn't have this problem."

"I didn't know then that I'd need a sitter, Kristy," my mother said. "Mrs. Randal didn't plan her heart attack in advance."

It was my turn to say, "Sorry."

I did a quick mental review of the schedules of the other members of the Baby-sitters Club. As president of the BSC, I usually have some idea if any of our club members is free to baby-sit.

Claudia Kishi, our vice-president, had a lot of homework that weekend, too. Claudia would be happy for any excuse not to do homework, though. I had to protect her from distractions — such as a baby-sitting job. So I couldn't ask Claud.

Stacey McGill, the BSC treasurer, was in New York City for the weekend visiting her dad. So she couldn't sit.

Abby Stevenson, our alternate officer, lives two doors down from our house, but she had a morning soccer game that day.

Mallory Pike, one of our junior officers, had a job baby-sitting for the Arnolds. And Jessi Ramsey, our other junior member, was rehearsing for a ballet performance at the Stamford Ballet School.

That left Shannon Kilbourne and Logan Bruno, our associate members. Associate members don't attend meetings or baby-sit as regularly as the rest of us. We call on them only when none of us can sit. But I knew Shannon had an out-of-town debate with the Stoneybrook Day School debate team, and Logan would be at football practice.

I was forgetting someone. It wasn't Dawn Schafer, a former BSC officer who lived in California now. Then I remembered. Mary Anne Spier — the BSC secretary and my best friend. As far as I knew, Mary Anne had no sitting job that morning. "Why don't you try Mary Anne?" I suggested.

My mother was lying on my bed and looking up at the ceiling. "Would you call her for me?" she asked. "This is such a comfy bed."

My mother's right about my bed. In fact my whole room is "comfy." It's huge and full of sunlight, like the rest of the house. Actually, our house is a mansion. It's three stories high, and has nine bedrooms, and a living room as big as a school gymnasium. Why do we live in a mansion? Well, my stepfather, Watson Brewer, is a real, live millionaire. When Watson and my mother married, our family moved in with him. His kids — Andrew (Batman) and Karen (the Joker) — live with us every other month.

I dialed Mary Anne's number.

Awhile back if I wanted to talk to Mary Anne I could have just yelled out the window. We grew up in houses next door to one another. The worst thing about moving into Watson's mansion was moving away from Mary Anne.

Mary Anne answered the phone.

"My mother wondered if you could sit for Karen, Andrew, and Emily for a couple of hours this morning," I said. "I have to work on my autobiography."

"Sure," she replied. I knew we could count on Mary Anne.

I told her that my mother would be over soon to pick her up. I said good-bye and hung up.

"Thanks, Kristy," my mother said. "I'll go for her in a minute. I just want to lie here a little longer."

I looked around my room. Emily and Andrew were still playing ball. Nannie was straightening out my pillows. Charlie was going through the pile of photos I had gathered for my English project. Shannon was chewing on the paper airplane I'd made for Emily. And, I remembered, Karen was still under my bed.

"Look at this," Charlie said. He showed me an old picture of him, Sam, and me with our father. I'm about Emily's age in the picture. Sam is standing on one side of our father and Charlie on the other. I'm sitting on our father's shoulders. "I remember when Mom took that picture," Charlie said. "We were having a picnic by the river." Charlie was actually smiling. The picture didn't make me smile. I don't like to be reminded of our father and all the happy times we had with him. That's because he's not around anymore. Our father abandoned us when we were just kids and David Michael was a baby. Dad didn't even say goodbye to us or anything. He just disappeared. We learned later that he moved to California and got married again. He doesn't write or visit like other divorced fathers do. My father hardly even sends me a card on my birthday.

"What are you doing with all these pictures, Kristy?" Charlie asked.

"I have to write my autobiography for English class," I told him. "It's due Monday." I looked around at all the people in my room. "I have to *work all weekend or I won't finish*," I announced loudly. "I might even *fail* English."

My mother sat up. "We should all get out of here and let Kristy do her work," she said to everybody. "Andrew, where's Karen? I'll bring you two with me to pick up Mary Anne. We can stop for an ice cream."

Karen's muffled voice came from under my bed. "Hooray! Ice cream!" Nannie and Mom jumped.

"Karen's been hiding there," I explained with a giggle.

Karen backed out from under the bed. Andrew shouted, "Catch the Joker!"

Nannie scooped up Emily so she wouldn't be caught in a Batman/Joker battle. And Charlie made a dive for Karen and held her high in the air.

"The Joker is captured," he announced proudly.

"We caught her!" Bath-towel Batman yelped.

The Joker giggled.

Shannon was leaping around the kids barking her head off.

"You guys!" I cried. "*Out* of here. All of you." But no one heard me. They were all laughing too hard.

A few minutes later I was finally alone and my room was quiet. It was time to work on my autobiography. I didn't mind doing it now, though. Seeing most of my big, crazy family in my room and thinking about the Baby-sitters Club reminded me that I had a wonderful cast of characters in my life story.

Thirteen Years in the Life
of Kristin Amanda Thomas

The First Five Innings

CHAPTER 2

Here's the story of the day I was born. It was a hot day in August about a week before I was due. My father and mother were going to a night baseball game at Yankee Stadium between the New York Yankees and the Boston Red Sox. Nannie baby-sat for my brothers — Charlie, who was four years old then and Sam, who was only two. I guess my mother thought going to a ball game would be a lot easier than staying home with my brothers.

My dad was a big Yankee fan so he was pretty excited about this game. And because he's a sportswriter he was always able to get great seats. When they reached Yankee Stadium they bought hot dogs and sodas and went to their seats. My father was ready to enjoy a great game under the lights. The one thing he hadn't counted on at this game was *me*. As soon as the home plate umpire yelled, "Play ball!" I let my mother know I wanted to see the ball game, too. She told my dad that she was having labor pains and that maybe they should go to the hospital.

"It'll be hours before the baby's born," he said. "Why should we hang around a hospital when we can be at Yankee Stadium?"

"You're right," she agreed. And they went back to watching the game. But my mom didn't enjoy it much. She was too busy keeping track of the time between her labor pains.

During the eighth inning my mother said, "Patrick, we *have* to go to the hospital. *Now*."

My dad helped my mother out of the stadium and drove her to the hospital. But they listened to the game on the car radio. At the bottom of the ninth the score was tied and the game went into extra innings. The game was still tied when my mother was admitted to the hospital. By then my dad was probably as in-

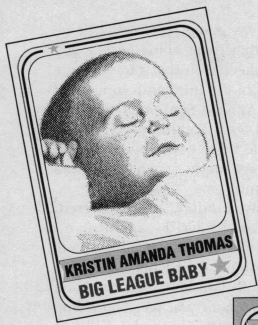

KRISTIN AMANDA THOMAS
BIG LEAGUE BABY

KRISTIN AMANDA THOMAS	
Stats:	
Drafted:	August 20
Time:	4 a.m.
Place:	Stoneybrook General Hospital (almost Yankee Stadium)
Average:	1.000 (Cuteness)
Future position:	Shortstop
Bats:	?
Height:	1'9"
Weight:	7 lbs. 2 oz.
Eyes:	Brown
Hair:	Brown
Hometown:	Stoneybrook, CT
Managers:	Elizabeth and Patrick Thomas
Teammates:	Charlie (4), Sam (2)
Personality:	Very active

You won't find my birth announcement in too many baseball card collections.

terested in who was going to win the game as he was in whether I was going to be a boy or a girl. (The Yankees won that game by one run in the bottom of the thirteenth inning.) If I'd been born in Yankee Stadium I bet they would have given me a lifetime pass!

Like most people I don't remember being a baby, so I asked my mother if she'd made a baby book about me.

"I'm sorry, Kristy, I didn't," she answered. "With three children under the age of five I didn't have time to write down all the cute things you were doing. I had my hands full just keeping up with you and your brothers. Kristy, from the moment you were born you were an active person, to say the least. I'd lie you down and those little fists would fly up in the air and you'd kick out your feet. We couldn't even keep a blanket on you."

I imagined myself as a squirmy, fussy baby. I've done enough baby-sitting to know that a fussy baby can be a real pain. "Was I fussy?" I asked my mother.

"Oh, no," she replied. "You weren't a crier, just a mover."

I asked Nannie what she remembered about me as a baby. "Did your mother tell you about when you took your first steps?" Nannie asked.

"Not yet," I said. "You tell me."

check out my great ball control!

"Well, even before you were ten months old you were pulling yourself up and walking around the edges of things, like your crib and the coffee table. One Sunday I came to your house for a visit. While your mother made lunch, I sat in the backyard watching you and your brothers. Charlie was teaching Sam how to play catch. You sat on the grass beside me watching the ball going back and forth. When your brothers moved out of your view, you grabbed my chair and pulled yourself up so you could see them. Just then the ball sailed past Sam and rolled to within a few feet of you. You let go of that bench and walked — no, you *ran* — to the ball. Then you squatted, without falling down, and picked it up. You're the only baby I've known who *ran* her first steps."

I don't remember all this, of course. My first memory is of being held up in the air and looking down at my dad's smiling face. He would toss and catch me and I would say, "Mo. Mo." (Translation: More. More.) I don't remember ever being afraid when my father threw me in the air. I must have trusted him. What a mistake. But more about that later.

Since I'm a person who is known for having brilliant ideas, I've been wondering when I started having them. The first one I remember came to me when I was almost five years old.

I was already best friends with Mary Anne and Claudia. Mary Anne and her father lived next door. (Mary Anne's mother died when Mary Anne was a baby.) Claudia lived across the street with her parents, her sister Janine (who is a real genius) and her grandmother, Mimi. Claudia, Mary Anne, and I played together whenever we could.

One Saturday I woke up to see the world sparkling with a heavy blanket of snow. I couldn't wait to be playing in that fluffy stuff with Claudia and Mary Anne. Our parents agreed that we could play in the snow together and that they would supervise us from their windows. It was a perfect day to be outside. The sky was clear, there was no wind, and it wasn't too cold. Many of our neighbors were shoveling their walks and driveways. My best friends and I ran around in my front yard, threw snowballs, made angels, and generally had the great time kids have in the snow. Then we made a snowman. While we played, Charlie was making money shoveling snow for our neighbors.

We were finishing up our snowman when Claudia told us that the next day was her grandmother's birthday. We all loved Mimi and decided we wanted to give her a present. But none of us had any money. I thought, If we were big enough to shovel walks like Charlie, we could make money to buy Mimi a present.

Our snowman turned out pretty well. Actually, it was a snow*woman*. She had a carrot nose, walnut eyes, a yellow tennis ball mouth, and a plastic flower wreath on her head. Several of our neighbors stopped to admire our snowwoman. One neighbor, Mrs. Goldman, said, "I remember when my nieces and nephews used to make snowmen. I used to love to look out my front window and see a snowman on the lawn." Then Mrs. Goldman climbed in her car and drove off.

We looked over at Mrs. Goldman's lawn. It was a blanket of pure snow. Not one footstep! "Let's make her a snowwoman," I suggested. Mary Anne and Claudia thought that was a terrific idea. We began at the edge of the lawn. Each of us made a snowball and rolled it toward the center of the lawn. As we pushed our growing balls, we walked behind them so we wouldn't mess up the rest of the snow. We met in the center of the lawn, then we piled the three balls on top of one another. It was time for the finishing touches. I ran to my house to get another old tennis ball and a baseball cap. Mary Anne raided her kitchen for more walnuts, and Claudia went to her house for the carrot.

As we were sticking the hat on the Goldman

snowwoman, Mrs. Goldman drove into her driveway. She jumped out of her car and exclaimed, "Look at that. You made me a snow-woman!" After admiring our work she handed each of us a dollar.

That's when my first really great idea popped into my head. "We can use this money to buy Mimi a present," I told my friends. "It'll be a surprise." When Mrs. Goldman heard what we were using the money for she gave us each *another* dollar! We weren't the only ones on Bradford Court who loved Claudia's grandmother.

"Hey, girls," Mr. Randolph called from across the street, "how about making one of those for the missus and me? We're having friends over for dinner and it would be a hoot to have a snowwoman greet them."

Claudia, Mary Anne, and I giggled. We were in the snowperson-building business! Mrs. Goldman helped us cross the street and we began rolling snowperson body parts on the Randolph front lawn. I noticed Mrs. Goldman on the sidewalk talking to Mr. Randolph. I'm sure she told him that we were trying to earn money for a present for Mimi, because when he gave each of us two dollars he said, "Now pick out something nice for Mimi. She's a special lady."

After lunch we were hired to make two more

The Snowperson Builders Club (SBC)
    President: Kristy Thomas
    Vice-President: Claudia Kishi
    Secretary/Treasurer: Mary Anne Spier

snowpersons. The first one was for Ms. Johnson. She helped us make the snowman, but she still paid us. "Mimi is terrific," she said. "When I had the flu last winter she checked on me every day. She did my grocery shopping, too." Ms. Johnson gave us ten dollars toward Mimi's present.

When we finished our last snowperson of the day, Mary Anne's dad said he'd bring us to Bellair's department store to buy the present. And Claudia's mother invited us all to a birthday tea for Mimi to be held the next day.

On the way to Bellair's we talked about what we should buy for Mimi. By the time we reached the store we had decided to get her a wool scarf to go with her black winter coat. "One with lots of beautiful colors," said Claudia.

Claudia and I thought that riding the escalator to the second-floor accessories department of Bellair's was a big thrill. Mary Anne was scared until I stood on her stair and held her hand. As those wide, moving stairs rolled us up to the second floor, I remember thinking, We're buying a birthday present for Mimi because *I* had a great idea!

We picked out a bright red-and-purple striped scarf. Afterward, Mary Anne's father treated us to hot chocolate and cookies.

It was dark by the time we returned to Bradford Court. But there was a full moon that made the snow and our snowpeople glow and glisten in the dark.

The next day Claudia, Mary Anne, and I presented Mimi with her present. We were rewarded with big hugs, thank-yous, and her wonderful smile.

Mimi wore that scarf every winter for the rest of her life. And it always reminded me of my very first great idea.

Breaking the Rules

CHAPTER 3

When I was little my brothers bossed me around a lot. I hated that. I also hated that they could do things I wasn't old enough to do. By the time I was five and a half I was pretty fed up with this situation. Sam and Charlie, who were seven and nine, were allowed to do so many things mom wouldn't let me do.

For example, Sam could cross our street to visit his friend by himself. I begged and begged to be able to cross to Claudia's house alone. My mother finally gave in. But by then, Sam was allowed to visit a friend on the next block all by himself, crossing an even *bigger* street to get there.

And here's something that bothered me every night. Sam and Charlie could stay up until nine o'clock — half an hour later than I could. When I finally got permission to stay up that late, their bedtime moved up half an hour, too. So I still had to go to bed before they did.

I must have understood at some point that I could never catch up. But that didn't mean I didn't keep trying.

I loved to play with Claudia and Mary Anne. But I wanted to play with my brothers, too. I liked the games they played — kickball, baseball, and a bunch of neat games with marbles. The trouble was that my brothers didn't want to play with me.

They would only let me play with them if they desperately needed one more kid to make a team. Or sometimes, when my dad was playing ball with them, *he'd* include me. "How's she going to learn if you don't play with her?" he'd say to my brothers.

Off to an early start.

"Aw, Dad, come on!" Charlie would say. "She's just a little kid."

"Besides, she's a girl," Sam would add.

"Don't let your mother hear you say that," my father would joke.

Then my dad, my brothers, and I would play a game of catch. Of course, I wasn't as good as my brothers. I was only five and a half years old, after all. But my dad would say things like, "Good catch, Kristy." And because he was nice to me, my brothers sort of were, too.

One of the things I had envied most about my brothers was that they went to Stonybrook Elementary School, while I went to preschool in the mornings and stayed at home with my mom in the afternoons. That changed when I started kindergarten at SES. Then every morning my brothers and I headed off to the same school. Of course Charlie and Sam never walked to school with me, but I still thought it was really neat that we were all at SES. They had a different opinion about the situation.

Charlie claims that I was always pestering him in the schoolyard. Claudia and I would march up to Charlie and the big guys he was hanging out with. I'd say something like, "Charlie, will you play catch with us?" Or,

"Let's play tag, Charlie. You can be It." (Mary Anne never did this. She was too shy.)

Charlie's pals would crack up. "Go on, Charlie, play with the little girls," one of them would say.

"How about ring-around-the-rosie?" another would tease. "Or patty-cake."

Charlie would go red in the face and say, "Beat it, Kristy."

His rejections didn't bother me. They were like water off a duck's back. Sort of.

Sam says I embarrassed him in front of *his* friends, too. I'd usually find him playing catch or kickball with his second-grade pals. Seeing those guys having so much fun made me want to play with them more than ever. Mary Anne and Claudia would play jump rope or something, but I'd hang out near Sam and his friends. If Sam saw me, he'd give me a dirty look and motion for me to go away. But I didn't care. And as soon as a ball was anywhere in my range I'd run for it, toss or kick it to Sam or one of his friends, and wait for someone to send it back to me. They never did. But I'd stick around anyway. If all I could do was retrieve their out-of-range throws, then that's what I'd do. I figured sooner or later they'd let me in their game.

My mother must have known how frustrated I was by being excluded from my brothers' activities. One day after school she tried to talk to me about it. "I think it must be very hard for you to be the youngest and the smallest in the family," she said. (This was before David Michael was born and long before I had two younger stepsiblings and Emily.)

I slid off the kitchen chair and stood as tall as I could. "I am not small," I proclaimed. "I am almost *five and three quarters* years old. Sam and Charlie are mean to me."

"That's right, Kristy," my mother said. "You are almost five and three quarters. But why do you want to do everything your brothers do? You have plenty of fun with Claudia and Mary Anne. And they're your age. Besides, it's more fun to play with someone who wants to play with you."

"I want to play with everybody," I said. "I want to play ball."

Just then Charlie came into the kitchen with a soccer ball under his arm. Sam was right behind him.

"What're you doing, squirt?" Charlie asked as he brushed past me.

"Nothing," I answered.

Sam went to the refrigerator, opened it, and swigged some orange juice from the container.

"What are you doing?" I asked Charlie.

"Playing kickball with the guys," he answered. "But you can't play with us, Kristy. So don't ask."

"Mom!" I pleaded.

"Come on, Charlie, let her play," my mother said. "Just this once."

"She's a little kid," Sam said with a burp.

"I'm already letting Sam play," Charlie told Mom. "He's the youngest. We have plenty of guys. Mom, we let her play with us lots. But not today, okay?"

My mother agreed that they didn't have to take me. Charlie and Sam left the kitchen with a bang of the screen door. When they were gone, my mother put her hand on my shoulder. "Try to understand, Kristy," she said. "Besides, you might get hurt with all those big kids."

"I don't care," I said. I felt tears well up in my eyes. But I didn't let myself cry.

"Why don't you go over to Claudia's and see if she wants to come back here to play," my mother suggested. "You can cross the street by yourself."

"Big deal," I mumbled.

Before I went over to Claudia's, I stopped in the bathroom to make sure my eyes weren't red from trying not to cry. But all I could see in the mirror over the sink was the top of my head. I was too short to see my whole face. My mother and brothers were right. I was little. I kicked the sink. Life wasn't fair. Why couldn't I have been the one born first?

CHAPTER 4

During the next week I made a mental list of all the things my brothers could do that I couldn't do. I called it *Things I Can't Do*. The list included: *Ride my bike in the road . . . stay up as late as the boys do . . . go to and from school alone . . . call friends on the telephone without asking permission . . . go to a friend's house after school without coming home first . . . play at the playground without an adult watching . . . drink juice and milk right from the containers . . . go to school without combing my hair.*

I don't think my mother even noticed that my brothers sometimes went to school without combing their hair, and she often scolded them for drinking from containers out of the fridge. But I *never* got away with either of those things.

By Friday my list was very long and I was more annoyed than ever about being the youngest in our family. Maybe that was the reason for what happened next.

It started after school when Claudia, Mary Anne, and I were waiting for Claudia's older sister, Janine, to walk us home. I noticed that my brothers were hanging out in the school-yard with their best pals, Rick and Randy Jones, instead of going straight home like me.

"Wait for me," I told Claudia and Mary Anne. "I'll be right back."

I ran to Charlie and Sam. "How come you're not going home?" I asked.

"We're going to a soccer game," said Charlie, "at the middle school."

"Then we're going to the movies," added Sam.

"My mother's giving us a ride," said Randy, "but we're going to the movies *alone*."

"We're gonna see *Car Man*," added Rick.

Car Man! I'd seen ads for that movie on television and everyone was talking about it in school. I wanted to see it more than anything.

To the mental list of *Things I Can't Do* I added: *Go to ball games after school alone . . . go to movies alone*. It wasn't fair. I was angry. I wanted to go to the movies, too. I was sick of being left behind.

As we were walking home I told Claudia and Mary Anne that my brothers were going

36

CAR MAN

At a theater near you!

my favorite superhero.

to a ball game and to the movies by themselves.

"All by themselves?" said Mary Anne. "I'd
be scared."

"Someday we'll be able to do that," said
Claudia.

"I'm going to do it *today*," I declared. "I just have to go home first. Then I'm going to meet Charlie and Sam at the game." When I said that out loud I knew that I was going to go to the soccer match and to see *Car Man*. I just didn't know how. By the time I arrived home I had a plan. I explained it in detail to Claudia and Mary Anne.

My mother was in the kitchen making lasagna for dinner. "Hi, sweetie," she said. "Do you want a snack?"

"No, thanks," I answered. I went straight to my room, opened my piggy bank, and took out all the money I had — two five-dollar bills. Then I went back downstairs.

"You sure you don't want a snack?" my mother asked. "We're eating a little later than usual tonight."

"I'll have a snack at Claudia's," I said. "She invited me to go to her house. Okay?"

My mother smiled at me. "Okay," she said. "Go ahead. Have fun."

I patted my jeans pocket to be sure the two five-dollar bills were still there. They were. " 'Bye," I called.

I walked out of the house. And then I ran down the block. At the corner I did something my brothers did that I wasn't supposed to do. *Cross big streets alone.* It felt great.

When I reached the Stoneybrook Middle

School playing field, the soccer game was already in play. Lots of people were in the stands. I couldn't find my brothers right away, but I wasn't afraid. Not for an instant. I was a big kid now, just like them.

I finally spotted Charlie and Sam sitting on the top row of the home-team bleachers with Randy and Rick. I climbed up and sat next to Charlie. The guys were pretty surprised to see me.

"What are you doing here?" Charlie asked.

"Kristy, go sit with Mom," Sam said.

"Mom's not here," I told them. "She said I could go to *Car Man* with you, too."

"Hey," Sam said. "Not fair."

"I've got money and everything," I said. I held up my two five-dollar bills. "I have enough money to buy everybody popcorn."

"Great," Randy said.

After the soccer match (Stoneybrook Middle School won), we met Mrs. Jones in the parking lot for a ride to the movies. She was surprised to see that I had joined the party. "My mom said I could," I told her.

"Well, I guess it's all right if you're with your brothers," she said.

When we reached the theater, Mrs. Jones told us, "I'm meeting a friend for coffee in the cafe right next door to the movie theater. Come find me there when the movie is over."

She waited until we'd bought our tickets. But once we were in the movie theater we were totally on our own. First we headed to the refreshment stand. We bought popcorn, sodas, and candy.

I felt great as I marched down the aisle of that movie theater holding a box of popcorn in one hand and a soda in the other. I wasn't a little kid anymore.

We found seats in the middle of the theater and settled back to eat and wait for *Car Man* to begin. Charlie got stuck sitting next to me, but he didn't seem to mind. A few of Charlie's friends came in and sat behind us. While he fooled around with those guys I ate popcorn and looked around at all the people in the theater. I decided I was the youngest person there who wasn't with an adult.

Then the theater darkened and the movie screen came alive with *Car Man*.

I loved the Car Man character. He was a superhero who could transform into a car whenever he wanted. Car Man had a secret identity as Todd Jones, used car salesman. The citizens of Biglee didn't know that Todd Jones was Car Man, the superhero who protected them from the bad guys. Here's the neat thing. Car Man didn't turn into the same car over and over. He could become any car he wanted.

It was a great disguise and a great way to do detective work.

About halfway through the movie, Car Man turned into a toy model car in order to spy in the hideout of his arch villain, Fire Breath. It was the first time that Car Man had turned into a model car. What he didn't know, and discovered right along with the audience, was that when he turned back into Todd Jones, he would be only four inches tall.

There wasn't a sound in the theater. Every kid held his breath as tiny Todd tried to hide from Fire Breath. I was terrified and loving it.

Just then the screen went blank and the lights went on.

Before anyone could yell out, "Hey, what happened?" a woman's voice rang out, "Is Kristin Thomas here?"

It was my mother.

CHAPTER 5

When I heard my mother shout my name in that movie theater, I slid as low as I could in my seat.

"Turn the movie back on," someone yelled.

"Who's Kristin?" someone else shouted out.

"Get her out of here," another kid shouted.

One of the guys in the row behind us stood up, pointed to me, and yelled, "Here she is!"

By then my mother was walking down the aisle. She spotted me and my brothers and stopped at the end of our row.

"Charles Thomas," she shouted. "What is Kristy doing here?"

"She said that you said — " Charlie began.

"And you believed her?" my mother asked incredulously. "Come on. You're all coming home with me."

"Mom, we didn't — " said Charlie.

"But Mom, it's Kristy's — " Sam whined.

"Now!" my mother said in the mother-voice

that didn't leave any room for disagreement.

The three of us stood up, squinched past the kids next to us, and followed our mother up the aisle.

Some of the kids we walked past were angry at us because it was our fault that the movie had been stopped. But most of them were laughing at us, which was even worse. Charlie hissed in my ear, "You're going to get it." And Sam gave me a little push.

Mrs. Jones was waiting for my mother in the lobby. "I'm so sorry, Elizabeth," she said.

"It's not your fault, Maxine," my mother told her.

"It wasn't our fault either," Charlie said.

"We'll talk about that when we get home," my mother snapped. "And not another word from any of you until I say so."

I walked next to my mother on the way to the car and made sure to sit in the front seat with her. I figured that was safer than being in the back with my brothers.

As soon as we arrived home, Mom told us to go to our rooms. "I'll speak to each of you separately," she said, "starting with Charlie."

I lay on my bed. I knew I'd be punished. I tried to distract myself from worrying about that by guessing what happened next in *Car Man*. Then I pretended I was Car Girl. As Car Girl I could turn myself into a big van and drive away from my stupid brothers and dumb-old-stupid Stoneybrook. I'd take Claudia and Mary Anne with me. If anyone tried to catch us, I'd keep turning myself into a different car. They'd never find us that way. I was in the middle of this Car Girl adventure when my mother walked into my room. She interrupted my Car Girl fantasy as abruptly as she had interrupted the Car Man movie.

Mom listed all the forbidden things I had done, starting with *You crossed a big street by yourself*. It was a long list. Finally, she said, "Do you have anything to say for yourself, Kristy?"

I knew she wanted me to say I was sorry. But I wasn't sorry about what I had done. I was only sorry I had gotten caught. So instead of apologizing and begging forgiveness I said, "How did you know where I was?"

"That's all you have to say for yourself, Kristin?" she asked.

I nodded solemnly.

"I asked Mary Anne and Claudia where you were," she explained. "Claudia pretended she didn't know, but Mary Anne couldn't do that."

I knew that Mary Anne could never tell a lie, even for a best friend. I wasn't mad at her. And I was glad that Claudia had tried to help me.

"It's a good thing that Mary Anne told me what was going on," my mother continued. "If she hadn't I would have had the police and fire department out looking for you. I was worried sick. I could hardly bear the thought of all the terrible things that could have happened to you. What if you were lost or had been kidnapped?"

I saw tears gathering in my mother's eyes. Suddenly I was sorry I had made her so worried and angry. I knew then with all my heart that what I had done was wrong. "I'm sorry, Mom," I said. "I am sorry I scared you. I won't do it again."

There was just one thing I didn't understand. Didn't Mom know I could take care of myself as well as Charlie and Sam could take care of themselves?

"The next thing we have to figure out is what your punishment will be," Mom said. "Your father and I will decide that when he comes home. But for now, you will stay in your room."

"Does Dad know I went to the movies?" I asked.

"Not yet," she replied. "He's covering an out-of-town football game. He'll know soon enough."

After my mother left my room I went to my window. Mary Anne was standing there watching me. She was crying her heart out. I smiled and made an okay sign with my thumb and finger so she would know I wasn't mad at her.

I lay down on my bed again. I tried to make up more adventures for Car Girl, but I couldn't think of any. My mind was too busy wondering what my punishment would be. I also wondered if my father would be as angry with me as my mother and brothers were.

When I heard my father come home, I opened my door and stuck my head into the hall to hear what I could hear. My mother was talking very seriously, but I couldn't make out exactly what she was saying. Then I heard my father laugh and my mother scold him for laughing. Then they started arguing. I knew it was my fault they were fighting.

Recently I asked my mom about that day. She said my dad thought what I did showed spunk and that I shouldn't be punished. She told him that she wasn't raising her daughter to be irresponsible. I think what she meant was she didn't want me to grow up to be irresponsible like him.

My mother won the argument, because before dinner she came to my room and told me what my punishment would be. "First, you may not go to Mary Anne's and Claudia's houses alone. If you're invited to their houses

I will bring you and pick you up. Also, your bedtime is now eight-thirty again. Lastly, your father is taking your brothers to see *Car Man* tomorrow. And you may not go."

"That's not fair," I protested. "How come they don't have a punishment?"

"You told them a lie," she said. "And they believed you. Do you think they should be punished for trusting you?"

"I guess not," I whispered. "But they're mad at me."

"They'll get over it," my mother said. "They weren't perfect when they were your age. And they still aren't. We all make mistakes, Kristy. And we all have to pay for our mistakes."

Well, I paid for my mistake all right. I hated having someone walk me to Claudia's house and even walk me next door to Mary Anne's. And going to bed at my old bedtime was boring. But worst of all, I wouldn't see the rest of *Car Man*. I would never know what happened to four-inch-high Todd Jones.

Saturday afternoon I watched out the window when my father and brothers left for the movie. Dad was kidding around with them. They were already having a good time. Then I thought, If only my brothers weren't mad at me I could ask them to tell me about the rest of the movie when they get home. And that was when I had another brilliant idea. But I would need Claudia's and Mary Anne's help if it was going to work.

I went downstairs to find my mother. "Mom," I said in a sad little voice, "can Mary Anne and Claudia come over and play with me?"

I guess she felt sorry for me, because she said yes right away. When Claudia and Mary Anne arrived I described my plan. They said they would help me. That it would be fun.

Two hours later, when my brothers came home from the movies, my friends and I were sitting in the middle of the living room floor playing with my collection of model racing cars and a bunch of dolls. We'd made a set for our characters that looked something like the *Car Man* set for Fire Breath's hideout. I had told Claudia and Mary Anne everything that had happened in the movie up to the moment my mother had interrupted it. That was when Charlie and Sam walked into the living room.

Sam said, "What are you doing?"

"Playing *Car Man*," Claudia answered.

I rolled a model car along the carpet. "Va-room. Va-room," I said in my Car Man voice. "I'll get you, Fire Breath. You won't hurt the people of Biglee City."

Claudia put a big doll's foot on top of the car. "Oh, yeah," she said. "How'd you like to smell my breath, Car Man?"

48

Every story needs a good ending.

"That's not what happened," Sam mumbled.

"Want to play with us?" I asked my brothers. I rolled the car toward Sam's feet. "You can be Car Man."

"Play with a bunch of dolls?" Sam said. "No way."

"They're not dolls," said Mary Anne. "They're actors in a movie."

"We're pretending the special effects and everything," added Claudia.

Charlie sat on the floor next to me. "Can I be Fire Breath?" he asked.

"Sure," I said.

Charlie tugged on Sam's pants leg. "Come on, Sam. You be Car Man. It'll be fun."

Sam sat down with us, too. My brothers aren't great actors, but we did learn how *Car Man* ended. Then we all made up our own Car Man story, with Car Girl and Car Boy. My best friends, my brothers, and I had a lot of fun that afternoon.

On Our Own

CHAPTER 6

When I was six years old everyone stopped treating me like a baby. There were some dramatic changes in our family life that year. One person joined our family and another person left it. The person who arrived was a baby — my brother, David Michael Thomas. The person who left was a grown-up — my father, Patrick Thomas.

The other day I asked my mother to tell me more about when my father left. She didn't really want to talk about it, but I told her I needed to know, not just for my autobiography but for myself. So we went to her room and closed the door.

She told me that during the years they were married she and my dad argued a lot. Sometimes he'd say things like, "I'm fed up with this life." Or, "I'd be better off without you and the kids." Then one night he didn't come home from work. He still wasn't home at midnight. Since he had stayed out late before she wasn't worried, just angry. But when she woke up in the morning, he still wasn't there. Then she was worried.

Mom called Dad's boss at the newspaper to ask if she knew where he was. His boss said, "Patrick quit. He told me he was heading west. I figured you were all going together, Mrs. Thomas. I'm so sorry." When Mom hung up the phone, she knew that my father had left her.

That must have been awful for my mother. She had four kids to raise on her own. And hardly any money. For awhile she hoped he'd come back, so she told us kids that Dad was away on business. But I knew something was seriously wrong. There were plenty of clues.

First of all, Mom cried a lot and would become angry at us for the littlest things. And when Mom's friends would come over for coffee and a visit, everyone would stop talking as soon as one of us kids would walk in the kitchen.

A couple of weeks after Dad left, Mom finally told us, "Your father has decided to live somewhere else. I'm sure he will call and talk to you about it soon." We had dozens of questions about this situation, such as *when* he would call us and *why* had he left. All she could answer was, "I don't know." Or, "I wish I could tell you that." And, "I'd like to ask him that myself."

Charlie was angry at our father. Sam was angry, too. But Sam was more angry at Mom than at Dad. One day Sam blurted out that it was her fault that our father left. She didn't scold him, but she went to her room and closed the door. Charlie was really mad at Sam. "She's probably crying again right now," he told Sam. "And it's your fault." My brothers usually got along pretty well with each other. But now it seemed they were always fighting.

I was sad and confused after Dad abandoned us. I wondered what I'd done wrong that would make my father want to leave me. Even David Michael, who was just a baby, noticed that his daddy was missing. He kept asking for *da-da*. During those first months after Dad left, David Michael and our new puppy, Louie, became best friends. I think my brother *needed* Louie.

One night, about six months after my father left, my mother asked us to meet her in the living room for a family meeting after dinner. "I have an announcement to make," she said. (We all started to talk at once, wanting to know what she was going to tell us.) "I'll tell you when we're settled in the living room," she said.

A few minutes later she was sitting in the rocker with David Michael on her lap. My brothers and I sat in a row on the couch. I was secretly praying that my mother was going to tell us that our dad was coming back. I was angry at him for leaving us, but I still missed him like crazy. Charlie had the same idea. "Is Dad coming home?" he asked.

"No," my mother answered. "What I have to say is not about your father." That's when I started to worry that something was wrong with our mother. What if she were sick and going to die? Without a father and mother what would happen to us?

My mother began by saying, "I've tried not to let your father's leaving affect you kids too much, but you must have noticed that things have been pretty tight around here without

The two new Thomases.

his salary. You also know that I've been looking for a job." We all nodded. "Well, I'm starting a full-time job in Stamford on Monday,"
she said with a big smile. "It's a terrific opportunity for me. And it pays pretty well."

"A job, Mom," said Charlie. "That's great."

I looked down at my worn-out sneakers.
"Can I buy a new pair of sneakers?" I asked.

"Yes, Kristy," she answered. "You finally
can."

"Can I go play now?" Sam asked.

Charlie stood up to leave the room.

David Michael wiggled out of Mom's lap.

I was about to ask if he could play outside
with me for a little while before it got dark,
when Mom said, "Sit down. This family meeting is not over." Charlie and Sam sat down.
David Michael was back on Mom's lap.

"This new job is great," Mom continued.
"But in case you haven't noticed, I have a full-
time job already — right here in this house.
How do you think I'll manage two jobs?"

"Gee," said Charlie. "Who's going to take
care of David Michael?"

"I've figured that part out," Mom replied.
"He'll go to a day-care center that's between
here and Stamford. I've already signed him
up. I'll leave him off on my way to work and
pick him up on the way back."

"So it's okay then," Charlie said. He stood up again.

"Not *all* okay," my mother said. Charlie sat down again. "I think I do a few other things around here besides take care of David Michael."

"Like cook," I offered.

"And wash our clothes," added Sam.

"Are we going to have a maid?" asked Charlie.

My mother laughed. "I'm not going to make *that* much money. I'll just about make enough to pay the expenses we have now. So, first of all, you guys are going to have to be your own baby-sitters. The three of you are to come right home after school each day."

Charlie and Sam moaned. (I had to come home right after school anyway, so it was no big deal for me.)

"Charlie," my mother continued, "you'll be in charge of Sam and Kristy."

"I can take care of myself," insisted Sam.

"Me, too," I added.

"The oldest will be in charge," my mother explained. "But of course you are all responsible for yourselves. I know it's been difficult for you kids these last few months, but you've been great. That's why I know I can count on you." Her eyes were filling with tears.

what's for dinner?

I gave her a hug. "Don't worry, Mom," I assured her. "We'll be okay."

"Who's going to cook?" asked Sam. "Charlie can't cook."

"I'll pick up take-out food on the way home," Mom said. "We'll have to eat a lot of take-out during the week."

"Good idea, Mom," Charlie said. "We can have pizza. Remember, I like it with onions."

"And anchovies on mine," said Sam. "Two slices."

"And we can have Chinese food sometimes, too," I added.

"I'm nervous about starting this job and leaving you guys," my mom said. She smiled at each of us. "But with kids like you I know it will be okay."

Boy, was Mom ever in for a surprise!

CHAPTER 7

Monday was Mom's first day at her new job. It was weird to see her come down to breakfast dressed up in a suit and high heels instead of old jeans, a sweatshirt, and sneakers. After breakfast she carried David Michael to the car. I carried her briefcase for her. I liked carrying that briefcase.

When she was behind the wheel and ready to go, I handed her the briefcase. "Wish me luck," she said. "See you tonight."

"Good luck," I called as she backed out of the driveway. She gave a little toot on the car horn and drove off. Charlie, Sam, and I were on our own.

Just then Claudia came across the street to pick me up for school. As we crossed the lawn to Mary Anne's I told her, "My mom started her new job today. Want to come over to my house to play after school?"

"Sure!" she answered.

mom starts her new job.

Our house was a very popular spot that week. Our friends loved the idea that we were on our own. Mom hadn't told us, "No other kids in the house after school." I guess in all the confusion of starting her new job, she forgot to tell us, or maybe she figured it was an unspoken rule. Mom was picturing her three darling children doing their homework and quietly waiting for her to come home with dinner.

Here's what we had to eat for dinner the first four nights of our new life:

Monday: Pizza
Tuesday: Chinese Food
Wednesday: Pizza
Thursday: Chinese Food

Mom didn't have time to buy regular groceries during the week. Or maybe she forgot. So by Friday morning there was no bread for toast. We were out of orange juice. And there was only enough milk for David Michael's bottle and Sam's cereal, which meant none for the rest of us. Charlie ate leftover sesame noodles cold from the container for breakfast. "Puke," I said. "How can you eat that for breakfast?"

"I left the fried rice for you," he said.

The idea of fried rice for breakfast made my stomach turn. I took a box of crackers and a jar of peanut butter from the cabinet.

My mother didn't seem to notice that there wasn't any breakfast food in the house. She was drinking a cup of coffee, feeding David Michael applesauce, and mumbling something about being on time for a meeting that began at nine o'clock.

Just then David Michael threw his bottle on the floor. Our puppy Louie jumped on it and bit into the plastic. Then he shook the bottle with his head, which sent the milk flying everywhere, including on Mom's suit. David Michael laughed. No one else did.

Sam pulled the bottle away from Louie and took him outside. Charlie cleaned up the milk mess. I finished feeding David Michael. And Mom went upstairs to change her clothes.

When Mom and David Michael were in the car and ready to leave, I handed her the briefcase. "Thanks, Kristy," she said. "You guys are being great. I'm really proud of how well you've taken care of yourselves this week."

"No problem, Mom," I told her. I thought, but didn't say, "It's fun."

On the way home from school that afternoon I asked Claudia and Mary Anne, "You coming over to my house again?"

"Okay," said Mary Anne. She was always happy for an excuse to get away from her baby-sitter.

a perfectly balanced meal.

"I'll bring candy," offered Claudia. "And caramel popcorn."

Snacks were one of the greatest parts of being on our own. Mom's idea of an after-school snack was an apple or a slice of cheese with crackers. She never let us have candy or super-sweet cookies. But our kids-on-their-own snacks were something else! By Wednesday we'd gone through all the sweet stuff in my house, including an old jar of Marshmallow Fluff and some stale leftover Christmas cookies. Claudia seemed to have an endless supply of junk food. I was never sure how she managed to have so much of it. I'm still not sure. I'm just grateful.

By four o'clock my friends and I were in my kitchen opening the bag of caramel popcorn. Charlie and Sam were in the living room playing a video game and eating their share of Claudia's candy.

Claudia ripped open the popcorn. "Oh, pew," she said. "This popcorn stinks."

I took the bag to smell it. That's when I noticed Louie scratching at the screen door to come in. I leaned over and pushed open the door for him. He ran in between my legs and I lost my balance. The bag of popcorn went flying. "Ugh!" I screamed. "It's *Louie* that stinks. What's that awful smell?"

Just then Charlie came into the kitchen, followed by Sam. "Something stinks," complained Charlie. "What is it?"

"Time to brush your teeth, Kristy," teased Sam.

No one laughed. By then we all knew what was stinking and why. We made a circle around Louie, who lay in the middle of the sticky popcorn spill with his chin on his folded paws. He looked ashamed.

"He's been sprayed by a skunk!" Sam exclaimed.

"He smells *awful!*" cried Mary Anne.

"We have to give him a bath," I declared.

"In tomato juice," added Charlie.

"Tomato juice?" Claudia and I said in unison.

"That's the way to get the skunk smell out," Charlie explained. "Shampoo doesn't work on skunk smell."

"How do you know?" asked Sam.

"Rick told me," answered Charlie. "It happened to his dog."

Tomato juice. I remembered seeing some tomato juice in the top cabinet when we were on a hunt for snacks. "We have two big cans of tomato juice," I said. I climbed on the stool to find them.

As I reached for the cans, a pile of paper plates and a stack of paper cups fell out of the cabinet and onto the floor. I would pick them up later, when I swept up the popcorn. First we had to get rid of that skunk smell. Skunk smell in a house is a lot stronger than when you drive past it in a car.

"We should wash him upstairs," said Charlie. "In the big tub."

Charlie grabbed Louie's collar and led him through the living room and up the stairs to the bathroom. Sam followed with a can of tomato juice. I carried the second can and a can opener. Mary Anne and Claudia followed me. We were holding our noses.

We had to close the bathroom door so all of

us could fit in there. I opened the window to let out some of the skunk smell.

"Charlie, how are you going to put Louie in the tub without getting skunk all over you?" I asked.

"That's a big problem," said Charlie.

"You could wear a garbage bag and gloves," said Claudia. She went down to the kitchen and came back with a brown plastic bag and the yellow gloves my mother used to wash dishes. Charlie cut holes in the bag for his arms and head. He slipped it on, then put on the gloves. Meanwhile I opened the cans of tomato juice.

Then Charlie put Louie in the bathtub and held him there. "Okay," he said. "Sam, you pour on the juice and I'll scrub. Then we'll rinse him. Kristy, you do that part." I attached the sprinkler Mom used for David Michael's shampoos to the faucet.

Louie stood perfectly still as the tomato juice flowed over and through his fur. But as soon as he was drenched in red he began to shake himself. Tomato juice flew everywhere — on the walls, on the sink, on us. Even on the ceiling. Two quarts of tomato juice is a lot of red stuff. We were all screaming and sort of laughing at the same time.

"Quick," screeched Charlie. "Rinse him off."

I turned a spray of water on Louie. Charlie and Sam did their best to hold him down while I rinsed him off, but still he managed to shake. Now water *and* tomato juice were flying around the room. By the time the tomato juice had been rinsed off Louie, everyone and everything in that bathroom was a red, wet mess.

"We better clean this up," said Charlie. "Go get some dishwashing liquid from the kitchen, Kristy. And some paper towels."

I was glad I was the one going on the errand. I couldn't wait to get away from the smell and mess of that bathroom. The only problem was that I couldn't leave. The door wouldn't open. "The door's stuck," I told the others.

"Let me try," said Sam. He did. "It's locked," he concluded.

Charlie tried the door. It wouldn't open for him either. "How could it be locked?" he asked.

"How do I know?" I replied.

"Unlock it," said Mary Anne. She looked frightened.

I pointed to the center of the knob. "The lock is stuck," I said.

"It won't pop out," said Charlie.

"You mean that little thing in the door-knob?" asked Claudia.

"Yeah," said Charlie. "Let's try jiggling it."

Peee — ew!

We all watched as Charlie tried turning the knob. But it wouldn't move.

"We're locked in!" Sam shrieked.

"Uh-oh," said Claudia.

I looked at Mary Anne. Any second now she'd start to cry.

"Stay calm, everybody," I said. "We'll just yell out the window for someone to come let us out."

I stood on the toilet seat cover and looked out the window. "I can see Mrs. Goldman weeding her front flower garden," I reported. I was about to yell to Mrs. Goldman for help when Sam grabbed my leg.

"Don't," he said. "Then Mom will think we were being irresponsible."

"And that we made this big mess," added Charlie. "We have to clean it up."

"What if we have to stay here forever?" Sam asked.

"It's like *jail*," Mary Anne gasped.

Claudia looked around the small, crowded bathroom. "There's no food," she said. There was panic in her voice.

Sam and I exchanged a glance that said, "We better take charge."

"You guys, don't worry," Sam announced. "We'll find a way to escape before we starve to death."

"I'll keep a lookout for someone to save us

who won't tell," I added. "You guys clean up."

They used all the toilet paper and our white bathroom towels. But it was hard for four people to move around that tiny bathroom, especially since wet Louie thought it was all a game meant to entertain him. When they were finished, the bathroom looked as if someone had had a blood bath in it instead of a tomato bath.

"It's like a horror movie," said Sam.

Just then I spotted Claudia's sister Janine coming home from the library with a pile of books. I didn't see anyone else on the street. We all agreed we could trust Janine. Claudia climbed up on the toilet seat next to me, and we yelled out the window, *"Janine!"* It took three calls before she figured out where the voices were coming from. But she finally saw us. We tried to explain with signals and words that we were locked in the bathroom.

"Here comes your mother!" shouted Janine. "I'll tell her."

"No!" we shouted.

But it was too late. Mom's car was pulling into our driveway and Janine was running toward it.

CHAPTER 8

W ell, there was nothing to do but wait for Mom to unlock the bathroom door. We heard her and Janine coming up the stairs. "What's wrong in there?" Mom asked in a nervous voice. Before we could answer she opened the door and saw her children splattered with what looked like a lot of blood. She let out a cry.

"Mom, it's okay. It's okay," Charlie said.

"It's only tomato juice," explained Sam.

Mom stared at us for an instant, then took another sweeping look around the bathroom. That's when she noticed Mary Anne and Claudia. "You girls go home now," she said quietly.

Mary Anne and Claudia left with Janine.

"Now you three go change your clothes," Mom said in an even, low voice. "Then meet me in the kitchen."

"It wasn't our fault, Mom," said Charlie.

"Louie got sprayed by a skunk."

"I figured out that much," she shot back.

"And we had to give him a tomato bath," added Sam.

"Why was Louie outside alone?" my mother asked. I looked at the floor. I was the one who let him out in the backyard to do his thing, instead of walking him on a leash.

"Sorry," I said.

Mom didn't say anything more, but left the bathroom with David Michael. Louie followed them.

"We're in trouble," said Sam.

"Big trouble," agreed Charlie.

"I guess we shouldn't have had kids over," I said.

"Or done a lot of other things we did this week," Charlie added.

We walked down the hall toward our bedrooms. The hall smelled of skunk.

Our mother's voice rose up the stairwell. "What on earth happened to this kitchen?"

I remembered the popcorn and paper plates. And that no one had bothered to wash the breakfast dishes.

My brothers and I ducked into our rooms to change our clothes.

When I came into the kitchen a few minutes later, Mom was calm. She was telling Charlie what cleaning supplies to use for mopping up the bathroom. "Kristy," she said evenly, "will you please clean up the kitchen."

"Sure," I answered. "I'm sorry we made a mess."

She ignored my apology. Sam came into the kitchen. Mom told him to set the table and watch David Michael. "The rest of last night's Chinese food is heating up," she said. "I'm going to change out of my business clothes. We'll eat in ten minutes." She went upstairs.

Charlie and I exchanged a glance. What was going on? Why wasn't Mom scolding us? Why wasn't she telling us what our punishment would be?

During dinner Mom said, "I take some responsibility for what happened here today. I've been so distracted trying to learn my new job that I wasn't clear with you kids about what *your* jobs are. That's going to have to change now."

That's all she said. Then she went back to eating her chicken and snow peas. So did we. But I was wondering, what does she mean by *our* jobs?

The next morning I found out. When I came down for breakfast I saw a long piece of paper posted on the refrigerator door. I looked at it. Mom had written down things each of us kids had to do.

Here was my list:

KRISTY

BEFORE SCHOOL:
make bed.
Put dirty clothes in laundry basket.
Put out milk and cereal for everyone.
Help Mom pack car for work and the
                        day-care center.

AFTER SCHOOL:
Do homework.
Fold clean clothes and put them away.
Set table for dinner.

WEEKENDS:
Dust all furniture in house.
Take care of David Michael when asked.
Do breakfast dishes.
Set table for dinner.

Sam's jobs included walking Louie after school, vacuuming the rooms and upstairs hall on Saturday mornings, and cleaning the kitchen after dinner.

Charlie had the most things to do because he was the oldest. They included cleaning the kitchen after breakfast on weekdays, scrubbing the bathrooms, doing the laundry, putting out the garbage, and giving David Michael his bath every night.

Charlie, Sam, and I clustered around the refrigerator door going over the list. Mom ate her breakfast and fed David Michael.

"Mom, this isn't fair!" Sam exclaimed.

"Excuse me," my mother said. "What isn't fair?"

He pointed to the list. "All this work. We're just kids."

"You'll still have plenty of time to play," my mother told him. "And as soon as we're settled into this work schedule I'll call some of your friends' parents and arrange play dates for you some days after school. But for the next few weeks I need to see that you kids can take care of yourselves *and* the house."

My older brothers and I moped around a lot that weekend. I had wanted to be treated as if I were older. But not *that much* older. I was also feeling nervous that I wouldn't be able to do all the things my mother had put on my list.

On Monday we started our new jobs. It didn't take much time to put out breakfast before school, or fold the laundry and set the table for dinner after school. Charlie and Sam did their jobs without too much trouble, too. We enjoyed the idea of surprising Mom with how well we could do everything.

When she came home that evening she had David Michael in one arm, a bag of groceries in the other, and her briefcase dangling from her hand. I took the briefcase, Sam took the bag of groceries, and Charlie took David Michael.

Mom looked around the kitchen in amazement. "This is great," she said. "I have a surprise for you, too. I bought a roasted chicken for dinner."

While Sam unpacked the groceries Mom put a pan of water on to boil for noodles and told Charlie to clean and cut the vegetables she'd bought. Fifteen minutes later we sat down for a real dinner.

I twirled some slippery, delicious noodles on my fork. "This is nice," I said. "I thought we'd only have pizza and Chinese food."

"We could have roasted chicken every Monday night, if you like," she said. "And we could figure out menus for other days of the week, too."

"I still like pizza," I said. "But once a week is enough.'

"Chinese food, too," added Charlie.

We all agreed that Chinese food on one night and pizza on another would be fine.

"And Charlie," my mother said, "if you could put some potatoes and a meatloaf in the oven one day a week that would take care of another night."

"I love meatloaf," I said.

"I could even make the meatloaf, Mom, if you showed me how," Charlie offered.

I looked around the table. Everyone was happy. Just then David Michael threw his bottle over the side of his high chair. Louie made a running leap for the bottle. I reached out and caught it in midair.

"Nice catch, Kristy," Charlie said.

"Not bad," agreed Sam.

"Thanks," I said.

Mom reached over and patted my head. "You're terrific, Kristy," she said. "You're really a big girl now."

Play Ball

CHAPTER 9

When I was ten years old we were still living on Bradford Court. By then my brothers and I were pretty good at taking care of ourselves after school and doing our chores around the house. Mom was working hard at her job in Stamford to support us. Once in awhile Dad sent a little money to help out, but it wasn't much.

It's hard to raise four kids on one salary, so we didn't have money for extras. That's why summers were a problem. Mom didn't want to leave us alone all day, but there wasn't enough money to pay for a full time sitter. She was always on the lookout for organized activities for us during summer vacation.

One Saturday a few weeks before school let out for the summer, Mom took a newspaper out of her briefcase and handed it to me. "Look at this, Kristy," she said. "Here's a girls' summer camp with lots of softball. It sounds like your kind of place."

I looked at the paper. The title of the article was: *Camp Topnotch: A Sporting Girl's Paradise.* There was a photo of a girls' softball team. The girl in the center of the photo held up a trophy topped by a statue of a girl winding up to pitch. The caption under the picture said that the Camp Topnotch softball team was All-Camp Winners in the junior girls' division for northwestern Connecticut. The caption ended with, "Will Camp Topnotch be the top team again this year?"

"Read the article," my mother said.

I sat down at the kitchen table and read every word of that article. Mom was right. Camp Topnotch was my kind of place. It specialized in softball, swimming, and tennis. If softball was your sport you could play softball almost all day long. There were games between cabins at the camp and games with teams from other camps. "It sounds great," I told my mother. "It must cost a lot of money to go there."

"You're right," my mother said. "It's too

expensive for us. But they give scholarships, especially to children in single-parent households. I called and they're sending us a scholarship application."

"Wow!" I exclaimed. "I really hope I can go." I looked at the article again and imagined myself holding up a trophy in the center of those girls. If I went to Camp Topnotch I'd make *sure* we won this year.

For the application I had to write an essay about why I wanted to go to Camp Topnotch. I said how much I loved the game of softball and that I was a really good shortstop. Then I wrote about how it was hard for a girl to find a good game in our town because the guys were sort of dumb about letting girls play with them. I also mentioned that my dad had left us, so my mom had to go to work every day plus raise four kids. I said I was proud of her for doing all that, but that it was really boring to be home alone in the summers. My mother answered the questions on the application that had to do with financial need. We mailed it in.

After that I checked our mailbox first thing when I came home from school every day. At the end of May I found a letter addressed to me from Camp Topnotch. I tore open the envelope, unfolded the letter, and read:

Dear Kristin Thomas:

Congratulations. We are pleased to award you a full scholarship for the month of July. Welcome to Camp Topnotch!

The letter went on to explain what day I should arrive and what clothes and sports supplies I should bring with me. There was even a map with driving directions to Camp Topnotch.

"Yess!" I shouted as I ran to the kitchen to find my brothers. "I got in," I announced breathlessly. "I'm going to Camp Topnotch. I can play softball for a whole month!"

"Big deal," Sam scoffed. "Who has to go to camp to play softball?"

"Hey, that's neat, Kristy," Charlie said. "You won a scholarship and everything. They must think you're pretty good."

"She's good enough to play with a bunch of girls," Sam said.

That's when it hit me. Camp Topnotch didn't know whether I was a good player or not. I had *told* them I was good. Now I'd have to prove it. I needed to practice.

For the next month I played softball every chance I got. After school, Mary Anne and Claudia threw balls for me to hit and catch. They wanted to help me any way they could. Sam and Charlie drilled with me, too.

The morning of July first I was suddenly nervous about going away to camp. I was going to be alone. No Mom. No brothers. No best friends. But Mary Anne and Claudia were both going on vacation with their parents in July. So I knew if I stayed at home I would be bored, bored, bored.

It took only a couple of hours to drive to Camp Topnotch. The towns we passed through were small, with just a couple of stores in each one. We mostly drove past open fields and woods. As we headed down the last mile of a bumpy dirt road it seemed that Camp Topnotch was *very* far away from Stoneybrook. Would I be homesick?

The countryside had been quiet, but Camp Topnotch was buzzing with activity. Everyone was friendly and I could tell that I wasn't the only girl who was a little nervous. One girl held her mother's hand, another was biting her nails, and I saw a girl clutching a teddy bear to her chest.

A counselor-in-training (C.I.T.) gave my mom and brothers a tour of the camp while another C.I.T. put my bags in a wagon and took me and my stuff to my cabin. "Your counselor will be there," she said. "You'll like her. Patti's great."

I wished my mom were coming with me to meet my counselor and see my cabin for the

Go, Bluejays!

first time. My stomach started to do little flips. What if I didn't like my counselor? What if I didn't like the other girls in my cabin?

The only person I noticed when I walked into the cabin was a short, happy-looking woman who looked quite a bit older than me, but not as old as my mom. "I'm Patti La-Pointe," she said, "your cabin counselor. Welcome to Bluejays' Nest, the *best* cabin in camp."

"Yess!" shouted a girl. The voice came from above me. I looked up to see a long-legged, red-haired girl sitting on one of the top bunks. She grinned down at me. "Hi," she said. "My name's Jillian Bilsky. But call me Jill." She jumped from the bunk to the floor. "I'm first base. How about you?"

I introduced myself. "Kristy Thomas. I play shortstop."

"Shortstop," repeated Jill. "Hey, cool. If you're better than Samantha Hunter you can be first-string shortstop on the camp team."

"Who's Samantha Hunter?" I asked.

"Sam's from the other softball cabin," Jill answered. "She was shortstop when we won the tournament last year. I was a second-string outfielder. But I'll be first string this year. You can bet on it."

"Pick out any bunk you want, Kristy," Patti said.

"Hey, take that bunk," Jill said. She was pointing to the top bunk nearest hers.

I'd never slept on a top bunk before, but I said, "Sure." I tossed my baseball glove on the bunk to show that it was mine.

It was Jill's second year at the camp. She helped me make up my bunk and showed me where to put my toothbrush and towel, and hang my bathrobe. Meanwhile, the eight other girls in our cabin were arriving and picking out their bunks. We all introduced ourselves and helped one another settle in. Most of the campers had been to Camp Topnotch before — only three of us were new campers. After awhile my mother and brothers came to see my cabin, meet my counselor, and say good-bye. I already had a good feeling about the camp and wasn't upset when they left.

When all the parents were gone, Patti said, "Well, campers, it's time to go to the mess hall and chow down. Our cabin sits at table five. I'll explain camp rules and stuff after dinner. Meanwhile, have fun and get to know one another."

Melissa, a girl I recognized from the newspaper photo, suggested, "Let's wear our colors for dinner so the Robins will know that we're ready to play ball."

"What colors?" I asked.

"Who are the Robins?" asked Tammy, another new girl.

Jill answered both questions. "There are two softball cabins," she explained. "We're the Bluejays. The cabin next to us are the Robins. Our cabins make up the teams that play one another during softball practice. For those games the Bluejays wear blue T-shirts or hats and the Robins wear red ones. It's sort of a camp tradition."

"Neat," I said. I rifled through my footlocker for my blue T-shirt.

When we walked into the mess hall I didn't have any trouble spotting the Robins' table. Every girl at table eight had something red on.

We sat down. The camp director, Mrs.

A little surprise for the Robins.

Spence, made a short speech welcoming us to Camp Topnotch. Then two girls from each table went to the kitchen to pick up platters and bowls of food. When Jill handed me the bread plate she whispered, "Watch the Robin on the end. The one with the red headband."

"Why?" I whispered back.

"Because she just put sugar on her potato instead of salt."

I watched the girl take a bite of her potato. She pulled a face that said, *Hey, this tastes weird.* Then she cautiously took another bite. Jill had to put her hand over her mouth so she wouldn't laugh out loud. The girl picked up the salt shaker, sprinkled some "salt" on the tip of her finger, and licked it. I saw her tell the other girls at her table that there was sugar in the salt shaker. They all looked toward our table. One of them gave us a thumbs-down sign.

"The war has begun," whispered Jill. Most of the girls at the Bluejays' and Robins' tables were smiling and kidding around about the prank, so I figured the competition between the Robins and the Bluejays was all in good fun.

I had trouble falling asleep that first night at camp. I was afraid that when I woke up I'd forget where I was, step out of bed, and fall five feet to the floor. Also, the country night noises were unfamiliar to me. The crickets were having a battle of the bands! But mostly I couldn't fall asleep because I was homesick. Homesick for my home and my family.

CHAPTER 10

The next morning I woke up to a trumpet playing reveille. As I climbed out of the bunk I remembered how sad and lonely I'd felt when I was trying to fall asleep. "It's a great day for softball," Jill remarked. Softball! Today I was going to play softball *all day long*. I wasn't sad anymore.

Our coach, Victoria Martin, was terrific. She started us off with calisthenics. By nine-thirty we were doing batting and fielding drills.

When I caught a pop fly on the run, Coach Martin shouted, "Good play, Kristy." I kept an eye on Samantha Hunter. She was a good player, too. But I made up my mind that this year I was going to be Camp Topnotch's *best* shortstop.

After lunch Coach Martin told us the positions we'd each play for our first Bluejays versus Robins game. She listed the Robins' positions first. I wasn't surprised when she said, "Samantha Hunter. Shortstop." Next, Coach Martin announced positions for the Bluejays. If only I could be shortstop, too. Then Coach Martin could see what a good player I was and then I'd have a chance of being the first-string shortstop for the camp team. I held my breath as Coach Martin read the names and positions. Finally, she said, "Kristy Thomas. Shortstop."

Yess! I thought. Jill and Melissa both patted me on the back.

Between the first and second innings Samantha and I passed one another in the field. "Hey, Shorty," she said, "how's it going?"

"Good," I replied. I punched my glove. "Real good. But my name's Kristy."

"Yeah," she said. "Listen, Shorty, I'm going to be shortstop for the camp team. So don't forget it, okay?"

"Break it up out there," called Coach Martin. "Let's play ball."

Samantha punched her fist in her glove and smiled at me. I didn't think it was a friendly smile.

I didn't let Samantha ruin the game for me, though. It was great to play with seventeen other girls who loved softball as much as I did. By the top of the seventh inning the Bluejays were down two runs. And Melissa — our best

nothing's getting by this shortstop.

hitter — was coming up to bat with two girls on base. Trouble was, when Melissa started walking toward the on-deck circle, she fell on her face.

A lot of us ran over to see if she was okay. By the time Coach Martin reached Melissa she was standing again and brushing herself off. "I'm okay," she said. "Tripped over my own two feet."

Everyone laughed, especially the Robins.

But Melissa lost her concentration because of that fall. She struck out and we lost the game. Softball was over for the day. It was time for free swim.

As the Bluejays walked back to the cabin to change into our swimsuits, the Robins skipped past us chanting, "We won because we won because we won because we won . . ."

I thought that was pretty obnoxious and said so to Jill.

"What's *more* obnoxious is *why* they won," Jill said.

"What do you mean?" I asked.

"The Robins tied my shoelaces together," Melissa explained. "When we were changing sides, a whole bunch of them started poking around the ground near the bench. They said they were looking for someone's retainer. What they were really doing was tying my shoelaces together. I didn't notice because Sam distracted me by talking about the game in that teasing way of hers."

"Did you tell Coach Martin they did that?" I asked.

"We *never* tell Coach Martin about this stuff," said Melissa. "It's between the Robins and the Bluejays."

Jill gave Melissa a little punch on the shoulder. "Don't worry, Melissa," she said. "We'll get back at them." And we did.

At dinner the Bluejays asked for seconds on buttered noodles. I snuck the refilled bowl under the table and dropped the noodles into a plastic bag. When the Robins climbed into their bunks that night they thought there were worms under the covers with them. You could hear their shrieks all over camp.

The next morning after breakfast Patti told us to "cool it on the pranks." But the night before I'd heard the Robins' counselor and Patti laughing about our prank. No one at Camp Topnotch was taking our intercabin pranks and rivalry too seriously. Not yet, anyway.

That afternoon during the practice game Samantha purposely got in my way when she was running to third and I lost the path of the ball. I made an error. I was furious at her. And

SCOREBOARD

	1	2	3	4	5	6	7
BLUEJAYS	0	0	3	6	8	14	17
ROBINS	0	1	5	7	8	10	10

A victory for the Bluejays, but not for me.

it's hard to play good ball when you're angry. I made another error on an easy ground ball in the seventh inning. Samantha was getting to me.

We still won that game by a score of seventeen to ten. "Good game, Robins and Bluejays," Coach Martin said. "Now go be fish for awhile. It's free swim time."

On the way back to our cabins, the Bluejays chanted, "We won because we won." Even though I had thought it was obnoxious when the Robins did that the day before, I shouted "We won" louder than anyone else.

It was a hot day and we were dusty and sweaty from playing ball. I couldn't wait to jump into the cool clean lake. The Bluejays raced one another around the cabin to the clothesline in the back where we'd hung our suits out to dry. The line was empty. "Maybe Patti put them inside," I suggested.

We went into the cabin. Our suits were no-where in sight.

"The Robins," muttered our pitcher, Rita. It took us ten minutes to find our suits. They were stuffed into Jill's pillowcase, all tied to one another in a big knot. A note was pinned to the tangle of suits.

Good Luck in the team tryouts tomorrow.

We were fifteen minutes late for afternoon swim. At dinner that night Mrs. Spence announced to the whole camp that the Bluejays were demerited ten points in the competition for Cabin of the Year. The Robins applauded. Mrs. Spence scolded the Robins publicly for their poor camp spirit and told the Robins to apologize to us. The whole Robin table said, "We're sorry, Bluejays." We knew that they didn't mean it, of course.

Before lights out that night, Patti gave us a lecture. "Girls," she said, "I can't understand how you could all be so late for swim period. Don't you want us to be best cabin? If we win, we can go to Splish Splash Amusement Park the second to last day of camp. Now come on, let's have a little team spirit here."

We told Patti we were sorry and that we'd try hard to win best cabin. I wasn't enjoying the pranks very much. I wished we'd stop playing them and concentrate on playing good softball. But the pranks weren't over.

When I got into bed that night I discovered that my bed had been short-sheeted. I curled up inside the little bit of space that was left for me under the blanket. I felt a piece of paper in there with my toes. I knew that a Robin had snuck into our cabin, short-sheeted my bed and left me a note. When I was sure Patti was asleep, I pulled my bedding apart and remade my bed. Then I got under the covers with my flashlight and read the note:

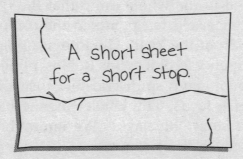

A short sheet for a short stop.

I couldn't fall asleep after that. I worried about whether I was a good shortstop after all. Being at camp with other girls who loved softball as much as I did was fun. But it also meant that I was with other very good players. I had to face the fact that maybe I wasn't as good a player as I thought I was, that maybe I wasn't as good as Samantha Hunter.

During softball practice the next morning we had more turns at bat than the other two days. Then Coach Martin hit some hard grounders to us. I missed two. Samantha didn't miss any.

After lunch we gathered around Coach to hear who would make first string for the camp team. "Okay," said Coach Martin. "Here's our team lineup. Everyone not on first string will be on the bench ready to come in at any time and to cheer the team on. I promise you'll all have the opportunity to play in the All-Camp games. Remember, we're not competing with each other. We're competing with other camps."

"Right," said Samantha. She winked at me. I didn't think it was a friendly wink.

Coach Martin read off the list of first-string players for Camp Topnotch. "First base. Jill." I gave Jill a congratulatory punch on the arm. I was really happy for her. Melissa was second base. Now if only I could be shortstop.

"Shortstop," Coach Martin finally announced. I crossed my fingers behind my back and held my breath. "Samantha Hunter."

"Oo-oh, too bad," Jill whispered. "I thought you'd get it for sure." That day I had to face the fact that Samantha *was* a better player than me.

Samantha walked over to me. "Tough luck, Shorty," she whispered.

I was thinking a lot of nasty things I'd like to say to her, but I just turned and walked away.

That night the Robins found two snakes in their cabin. Believe it or not, the Bluejays didn't put them there. But we took credit for it anyway.

Camp Topnotch won the first All-Camp game. I kept my eye on the action, especially at shortstop. I had to admit to myself that Samantha Hunter was a terrific shortstop. I was beginning to think that coming to Camp Topnotch hadn't been such a good idea after all.

CHAPTER 11

Our softball schedule for the next two weeks included six All-Camp games. Coach Martin put me in the outfield for a couple of innings each game, but it was boring compared to being shortstop. And being on the bench for the rest of the innings was *very* boring. We won three games and lost three. Coach Martin thought we should have won all of those games. She kept giving us speeches about team spirit. But it didn't do any good.

The problem with our camp team was that we were still involved in the Robins versus Bluejays competitions. We were more interested in the outcome of our pranks and the games between the Bluejays and the Robins than in the All-Camp games.

In the van on the way to our seventh game Coach Martin gave us another pep talk. "Look, I don't feel a team spirit here. To win you've got to play together as a team. It isn't Robins versus Bluejays anymore. You're all on the same team."

We lost our seventh All-Camp game.

In the van on the way back to camp, Robins and Bluejays blamed each other for the loss. The team pitcher (a Bluejay) blamed the catcher (a Robin) for giving her misleading signals. The shortstop (a Robin) blamed the first baseman (a Bluejay) for a wide throw to second, ruining a possible double play.

We went from that argument to arguing about which cabin team was better, the Robins or the Bluejays. We compared scores from the games we'd played against one another and said things such as, "We're going to *kill* you the next time. Just wait and see." And, "You couldn't hit a T-ball."

Most of the times when kids talk like that they're kidding. The Bluejays and the Robins were *not* kidding.

During our argument Coach Martin was leaning back with her eyes closed. I figured she was taking a nap, but I soon realized she must have heard every word. As the van turned onto the dirt road that led to camp, Coach Martin suddenly jumped up and asked the driver to pull over and stop the van.

"What happened, Coach Martin?" Alicia yelled.

Jill mumbled, "A Robin probably put sand in the gasoline tank."

Coach Martin stood in the aisle and stared at us. She was silent and stern.

The girls were calling out questions. "Hey, Coach Martin, what's up?" And, "Why are we stopping?" And, "Is the van broken?" Coach Martin didn't answer any of our questions. Finally, we all quieted down and waited to see what would happen next.

Coach Martin spoke in a quiet voice, but you could tell she was angry. "I've talked to this team about team spirit until I'm blue in the face," she began.

"See, Coach Martin is a *Blue*jay," someone called out. A few Bluejays laughed. Coach Martin didn't. We were quiet again.

"You girls are more interested in beating one another than in beating other teams," she continued. "No team plays its best when there's in-fighting. Believe me, it is no fun to coach a team that acts the way you do. It is no fun to watch your games, either. I am ashamed of your behavior. So guess what. I don't want to have anything more to do with this team. I quit as your coach."

"What about the rest of the All-Camp games?" someone called out.

"Mrs. Spence can assign someone to go with

you to your games or she can withdraw the team from the competition. I don't care. I'm not going with you."

"Aw, come on, Coach Martin," someone shouted. "Don't do that."

Coach Martin told our driver that she'd walk back to camp. Then she pushed open the van door and left.

As soon as she was gone everyone started talking. Bluejays blamed Robins for not keeping the pranks secret. And Robins blamed Bluejays for bragging in front of Coach Martin about their wins in our intercabin games. I didn't say anything. I was feeling pretty rotten about Coach Martin's quitting. I was feeling pretty rotten about everything at Camp Top-notch. I wanted to go home.

We went back to our cabins to change out of our sweaty, dusty uniforms. Since we'd been on our softball trip during mail call, Patti had put our mail on our pillows. I could see I'd gotten something. I climbed up on my bunk to read what I thought would be another letter from my mother. But it wasn't a letter, it was a postcard with a picture of a carousel. I turned the card over. It wasn't from my mother. It was from Mary Anne.

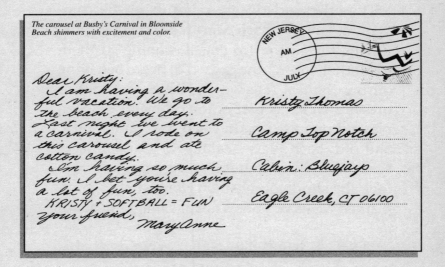

The carousel at Busby's Carnival in Bloomside Beach shimmers with excitement and color.

Dear Kristy:
I am having a wonder-
ful vacation. We go to
the beach every day.
Last night we went to
a carnival. I rode on
this carousel and ate
cotton candy.
I'm having so much
fun. I bet you're having
a lot of fun, too.
KRISTY + SOFTBALL = FUN
your friend,
Mary Anne

Kristy Thomas

Camp Top Notch

Cabin: Bluejays

Eagle Creek, CT 06100

Mary Anne doesn't know how much this card meant to me.

"Your friend, Mary Anne." I was suddenly sad and lonely. I missed my best friend. I thought about how kind Mary Anne was. I knew that if she were at Camp Topnotch she'd hate all the fighting between the Robins and the Bluejays.

I read the card again. As I read, "Kristy + softball = fun" I thought, I'm not having any fun playing softball. I remembered what Coach Martin said to us in the van. "It is no fun to coach a team that behaves the way you do. It is no fun to watch your games."

107

The other girls in my cabin were still complaining about Coach Martin and blaming the Robins for all the trouble. Listening to them reminded me of the way I'd been behaving during the last few weeks. I had to admit to myself that I was part of the problem. I'd been playing pranks, I hadn't had any camp spirit, and I'd been very jealous of Samantha. I wasn't proud of myself. "And look how Sam took the shortstop position from Kristy," complained Melissa. "She's always bragging about it."

"Hey, Kristy," Jill said. "What was that mean thing Sam said to you today?"

I was about to repeat a stupid insult that Sam had made during the game with Camp Buckley, but I stopped myself. Instead I said, "You guys, what are we going to do about our coach? It's serious when a coach quits."

"Yeah, it is," agreed Melissa. "And she's a great coach."

"We haven't been acting like a great team," I said. "Let's have a meeting and figure out what we can do to straighten things out and make softball fun again."

"It'd be *fun* to play a bunch of games against the Robins and show everyone who's the best once and for all," said Tammy.

"But we're supposed to be playing for the

camp," I said. "That means *working* with the Robins, not always fighting with them."

"Kristy has a point," said Jill.

"The only way we can fix things is if the Robins and Bluejays work together," I said. "That means we have to sit down and talk with them about what's been going on."

"The Robins want to have a meeting with the Bluejays, too," said a voice from the door. We looked over to see Sam and the other Robins standing at our door.

"It was our idea to have the meeting first," one of the Robins piped up.

"Hey, guys," I said. "That's not the point. We have to stop that stuff."

"Right," said a voice. I didn't even bother to think about whether it was a Bluejay or a Robin who said it.

Jill suggested we go outside and sit in a circle in the area between our two cabins and have a meeting. Sam suggested that we invite our counselors to help us iron things out. At the meeting we all had a chance to talk.

That evening the Robins and the Bluejays walked into the dining room . . . *together*. All talking stopped. The other campers were watching us. Instead of going to our tables we walked straight to where Coach Martin was sitting. Sam and I, as representatives of our joint cabins, handed her a petition that read:

Dear Coach Martin:

    We the undersigned apologize for our unsportsmanlike behavior. We are sorry. We want you to come back as our coach. If you do, we promise that we will play with total team spirit. Please give us another chance.

a peace treaty

Everyone in the two cabins had signed that petition. Coach Martin read it, thought for a moment, then said, "I'll watch your practice tomorrow. I won't give you any instructions. I'll just be an observer. Then I'll decide."

The next day when we met at the ball field for our drills and practice game, one girl from each cabin chose up teams that weren't one cabin against the other. Samantha and I were on the same team. She played shortstop and I played second base for the first half of the game. Then we switched positions. Sam gave me some pointers and we made some awesome double plays in that game.

Camp Topnotch was too many games down in the All-Camp games to win a trophy. And both the Bluejays and the Robins had too many demerits to have any chance of winning best cabin. But The Birds — as we now called our two cabins — had a great time during the last week of camp. And we played a lot of good ball. I learned that you don't have to be the best at something to have a good time. And guess who turned out to be my best friend at camp? Samantha Hunter. I was really glad that I went to Camp Topnotch after all.

Guess who ended up being my best friend at Camp Topnotch.

My Real Father

CHAPTER 12

I haven't written much about my father in my autobiography so far. An autobiography is about your life, and my father hasn't been in my life that much. Other kids I know whose parents are divorced spend time with both parents. After my parents were divorced, my father never even wanted to see his kids.

He knew where we lived, so he could have found us if he wanted to. And when Mom married Watson Brewer and we moved from Bradford Court into Watson's mansion, she sent Dad a letter telling him our new address, just in case he wanted to send her a child support payment (ha!) or get in touch with his children (double ha!).

Our father did send us a few birthday cards and postcards over the years. The postcards said the same thing: "Hi. Expect to be out east this month. Will call. We'll get together. Love, P."

Notice the signature: "P." You might think it stands for *Pop* or *Papa*. It doesn't. The "P" stands for "Patrick." I guess it's hard to call yourself "Pop" or "Papa" when you never see your kids. I sometimes wondered if Patrick Thomas felt like our father.

Last spring we received another postcard from Patrick. It said the same thing as the others — that he was coming east and he'd see us. Since "P" had never come before, I didn't believe he'd come this time.

But guess what? "P" actually showed up. There he was one day — on a street corner in Stoneybrook calling my name. I didn't recognize him at first. After all, I hadn't laid eyes on the man in six years. When I realized who he was, the angry feelings I had toward him bubbled up inside me. But I was still excited and glad that he was there. I'd missed him during those six years.

I asked Patrick a lot of questions and found out that he and his California wife had split up. He said he wanted to move back to Stoneybrook. He also said that for the time being he only wanted to see me and not the rest of the family. I asked him why. He explained that he wanted to wait until he was settled. But in the meantime, he wanted to spend some time with his only daughter.

After that Patrick and I started meeting secretly. I was glad that Sam and Charlie were on a camping trip. It would have been hard not to tell them. It was difficult enough not to tell Mom and my friends. But there was one person who knew my real father was in town: Mary Anne. She was with me the day Patrick and I were reunited. I made her promise that she wouldn't tell anyone else. I was happy that Mary Anne knew about my secret life with my father. Otherwise I wouldn't have had anyone to talk to about it.

Meanwhile, I was lying to everyone else to cover up for the times that I saw Patrick. I'd say I was going to a friend's house or on a baby-sitting job, then I'd sneak off to meet him. We had a lot of catching up to do and shared lots of stories.

One afternoon over pizza he told me all about his years as a baseball player for a minor league team. "I'm a pretty good softball player myself," I said. "I guess I inherited your talent." Then I told him about Kristy's Krushers. He thought it was pretty neat that I coached a team and he laughed like crazy over some of the stories I told about the kids at our games, especially the ones about Jackie Rodowsky, the Walking Disaster.

Then he told me about some pranks he and his teammates used to play on one another. The pranks sounded a little juvenile — like the ones the Bluejays and Robins pulled at Camp Topnotch — but they were funny anyway. There was no way around it. Patrick was a fun guy.

The day after Patrick and I had the pizza, Mary Anne walked me to a baby-sitting job at the Rodowskys' on the way to her job at the Johanssens'. I told her about my time with Patrick and all the things we talked about. I figured she'd crack up when I told her about the pranks he used to play on other ball players. But none of the stories made her laugh, even the one about the time Patrick put itching powder in a buddy's pants the night he had a big date. "It's funny, Mary Anne," I said.

"Your father likes to joke around a lot, doesn't he?" Mary Anne said. She looked worried.

"If you're thinking he's irresponsible, why don't you come right out and say it?" I asked.

"I wasn't thinking that," she said. "I just don't understand why he won't let you tell anyone that he's here. It doesn't seem like a very grown-up way to handle things."

"I told you why," I said impatiently. "It's not so hard to understand."

"Well, I still don't understand," she mumbled.

"Well, I do," I countered. "And it's all going to work out great." Actually, a big part of me agreed with Mary Anne. It really bothered me that my father didn't want anyone else to know he was in town. But the other part of me was so happy to be with him again that I tried to forget about that. There was so much about my father that I liked. Even if he did act a little immature sometimes, he was always cheerful and full of fun. I imagined my very own dad at a Krushers softball game, cheering my team. I pictured him taking all my friends for pizza and telling them some of his funny stories. Then, I thought, Mary Anne will see that he's a great guy.

We'd reached the Rodowskys'. I couldn't wait until I saw my father again. I wished I were meeting him right away instead of after my baby-sitting job.

"Well, here we are," I said.

"Call me if you want to talk or anything," Mary Anne offered. " 'Bye."

The Rodowsky boys were wilder than ever that evening, especially Jackie. But finally they all went to sleep. A little later Mr. and Mrs. Rodowsky came home. I told Mrs. Rodowsky how the evening had gone and she handed me my pay. "Thanks, Kristy," she said. "It's wonderful to know that we can depend on you. My husband is waiting in the car to take you home."

"Mr. Rodowsky doesn't have to give me a ride tonight," I told her. "I have a ride." Not a lie. I just didn't tell her *who* was giving me a ride.

When I got outside I could see Patrick's car parked at the end of the block. Mr. Rodowsky was waiting for me in his car. I told him that I had a ride.

"Okay," he said. He got out of the car. "I'll wait with you until they come."

"Ah — I'm meeting them at the corner," I said.

"Well, I'll walk you to the corner and wait with you," he said.

If Mr. Rodowsky walked me to the corner
I'd have to introduce him to my father. Otherwise it would look weird and rude. Time for
a lie. "My brother Charlie is coming for me,"
I said. "His car's broken and he borrowed his
friend's car." I pointed to the car at the corner.
"There they are now. Gotta go. 'Bye." I turned
and ran.

When I reached the car, I jumped in and
banged the door shut. "Let's go," I said. I felt
like a criminal making a getaway.

"Hi, there," Patrick said. He started the
motor. "How'd you like to go bowling in
Stamford?"

"I can't," I said. "I told Mom I'd be home
by ten. It's already after nine-thirty."

"So tell her you had to sit late," he said.

"If I don't come home on time she'll call the
Rodowskys. They'll tell her when I left their
place. And I sort of just lied to them about
who was picking me up. I'll be in big trouble
with Mom and she'll find out you're here."

"You poor kid," he said. "Elizabeth sure is
keeping you on a short leash." He put his
hand around his neck and pretended a collar
was choking him. "I lived with Elizabeth. I
know how it feels."

"I don't like it when you say things like that
about Mom," I said. "It was hard on her, the
way you left and everything."

He shifted into gear. "I suppose," he said. "But she was always better than me with that domestic stuff." I didn't say anything. I wondered if my father was angry at me for criticizing him.

"Look, Kristy," he began. "I'm sorry I've been such a lousy father to you. I'm trying to make it up. I'm doing the best I can. Give me half a chance. Okay?"

"Sure," I said. "That's cool. I'm glad you came back . . . Dad." That was the first time I called him "Dad." He grinned at me to let me know he liked that. I hoped it made up for criticizing him.

"How about we swing in through the drive-in joint and get something to eat?" he suggested. "Do you have time for that, Cinderella?"

"You better bring me back on time," I kidded, "or your car will turn into a pumpkin."

Dad reached over and pulled my hat over my eyes. "Guess you've got your old man's sense of humor."

I pushed my hat back. "Yeah," I said, "I guess."

I leaned back in the seat and watched the night flow by. I was glad my dad was back.

CHAPTER 13

Over the next week I met my father as often as I could. We went bowling in Stamford one day. Another time we had a picnic at the river and he taught me how to play a card game called hearts. We were having fun together and I was getting used to calling him Dad. But he still wouldn't let me tell anyone that he was in Stoneybrook. I had to continue to make up stories about where I was going and what I was doing. As a result, I wasn't handling my responsibilities with my usually efficiency. It's hard to be responsible when you're leading a secret life and lying all the time.

On Saturday morning I was supposed to meet Dad for breakfast. We planned to spend the whole day together. He said he had a surprise for me and I couldn't wait to see what it was. Maybe he'd tell me that he found a job and I could help him pick out an apartment. I wondered if I'd have my own room at his

Patrick can be so much fun.

place, like Stacey and Dawn did at their fathers' places.

I dressed and went downstairs. I wanted to leave the house before anyone could ask me how I was spending the day. I hated lying. By some miracle no one else was in the kitchen. My stomach rumbled. I decided to have a quick glass of juice before I left. But Mom came into the kitchen. "Morning, honey," she said.

"Morning, Mom," I answered.

She poured herself a cup of coffee and sat down at the table. "I'll have some more coffee and keep you company while you eat your breakfast. It'll give us a chance to talk. I haven't been alone with you in days."

I was trapped. I sat at the table across from Mom.

"How've you been?" she asked.

"Great," I said. "Really busy."

"I noticed. Is everything all right with the Baby-sitters Club?"

"Yeah," I said. "Great."

"So everything's great?" she said.

"Yeah," I repeated. I drank the last of the juice.

And Watson came into the kitchen. "Morning, Kristy," he said cheerfully. "How's it going?"

"Great," I replied.

He and Mom exchanged a glance that said neither of them believed me.

"Well, eat a good breakfast," Watson told me. "You're going to need your strength to tackle that lawn."

The lawn! I'd completely forgotten about it. I'd put off my lawn mowing job every day that week. Now it was Saturday and I'd promised Watson I'd do it on Saturday for sure. I had hoped to spend the whole day with my dad. Now I'd have to come home and mow that stupid lawn.

"I have to baby-sit this morning," I lied. "But I'll do the lawn as soon as I come home."

"You're a hard worker, Kristy," Watson said. "Baby-sitting, coaching the Krushers, and doing your share at home." He patted me on the shoulder. "Good for you."

"Thanks," I said. Watson was always so nice to me. It made me feel doubly rotten about lying to him.

"Do you need a ride to your baby-sitting job?" he asked.

"No, thanks," I said. "I'll ride my bike."

"Who are you sitting for?" my mother asked.

"The Barretts," I answered. Another lie.

I rode my bike at top speed into town. I was meeting Dad at Thelma's Cafe. We had picked

Thelma's as a meeting place because no one I knew went out to breakfast on Saturday morning.

Dad wasn't in Thelma's so I stood outside and waited for him. I was looking up and down the block when I noticed Watson's car pulling up in front of the cafe. He saw me before I had a chance to hide, and he got out of the car and came over to me.

"You followed me," I said. "Are you spying on me?"

He looked confused. "I didn't follow you. I happened to drive by and saw you standing here. I stopped to tell you not to worry about the lawn if you have to work late. I'll probably have time to do it later myself."

"That's all right," I said. "I can do it."

Watson looked around. "Where are the Barrett kids?"

I was stumped for a second. Then I thought, I'll tell him Mrs. Barrett is meeting me at the cafe with the kids and she's late. But before I could tell my newest lie, Watson said, "What's wrong, Kristy? You look like a trapped animal. You aren't baby-sitting this morning, are you?"

I couldn't tell another lie. I just couldn't. I shook my head no. "But I'm not doing anything wrong, Watson," I said. "Really, I'm not. I just can't tell you anything yet. Please, please, don't tell Mom that I'm not baby-sitting."

"Are you in trouble?" he asked in a worried voice.

"No," I answered. "It's nothing bad. Really. I promise I'll tell you and Mom everything as soon as I can."

Watson looked me in the eye. "I only want what's best for you, Kristy," he said. "You know that. At least tell me what I can do to help you."

"What you could do for me right now," I said, "is to not ask me any more questions, and leave." I pleaded with my eyes.

Watson thought about it for a second. "All right," he said. He got back in his car and drove away.

My father didn't show up for another half hour. I pointed out that he was late, that he said we'd meet at nine and it was nine-thirty.

"I overslept," he explained. "You should have come by the hotel and told them to give me a wake-up call."

"I didn't think of that," I admitted. I noticed he had a softball glove tucked under his arm. When he noticed me noticing it, he handed me the glove and grinned. "Here's your surprise," he said. "It's a present for some of those birthdays I missed."

Nice try, Dad.

"Thanks, Dad," I said. "Thanks. I needed a new glove. How did you know?"

"I guess I know my girl pretty well," he said.

"It's perfect." I was so happy. The leather felt wonderful. And I could tell it had strong stitching that would hold up to abuse. I thought of my worn-out glove with the torn stitching. I *needed* a new glove. And my dad knew it. I was about to put the glove on, but I stopped in mid-gesture. It was a right-handed glove. I was a lefty. I couldn't believe it. Didn't he even know that I was left-handed? I was speechless.

"Isn't it a great glove?" he said. "Only the best for my girl."

"Great," I said, even though his present was all wrong.

I didn't tell Dad that he bought his left-handed daughter a right-handed glove. How come he didn't remember that about me? I wondered.

"We'll play some catch this afternoon," he suggested. "You can break in your glove."

"I have to go home and mow the lawn," I told him.

"That short leash again," Dad said with a grin. He made the choking gesture again. I smiled even though I didn't feel like it.

CHAPTER 14

When my father and I were settled in a back booth at Thelma's, I told him that I'd thought my surprise was that we could finally tell Mom and everyone that he was in Stoneybrook. "I thought maybe they gave you the job you've been talking about," I added.

"That's coming along," he told me. "Don't worry your pretty head about it."

During breakfast we exchanged stories about the places we'd traveled to and which ones were our favorites. Actually, he did most of the talking. Whenever I mentioned a place I'd visited, such as Florida, he'd interrupt to say something like, "If you think Florida is interesting, you should go to Mexico." Then he'd tell me all about a trip *he* took to Mexico.

It made me wonder, If he could go to all those places, how come he never came to see me?

After breakfast we went to his hotel and

played hearts in the lobby. I didn't care much about playing cards that morning. I kept thinking about the softball glove and how he didn't even remember I was a lefty. Then I started thinking about how he deserted my mother and us kids without any warning. I tried to put those thoughts out of my head and concentrate on the card game, but Dad could tell my mind was someplace else.

"Penny for your thoughts?" he said.

"They're worth a lot more than a penny," I replied.

He grinned. "There's an idea," he said. "Let's play cards for pennies."

"I have to go now," I said. "The lawn."

"Lawns," he chortled. "I never could understand people's obsession with cutting grass. Why can't they leave the poor grass alone. Who cares if grass is long?"

"Lots of people, I guess," I answered. I didn't feel much like discussing lawns with my father. Or anything else, for that matter. I was in a rotten mood.

During my bike ride home I thought, Maybe Dad should be excused for not remembering — or noticing — that I'm a lefty. After all, he hasn't seen me in six years. Then I remembered how he always brought the conversation back to himself and I thought, Maybe I didn't talk much at breakfast because of the whole glove thing. Maybe I'm in a bad mood because of all the lying I've been doing.

By the time I rode my bike up our driveway I'd decided that my relationship with Dad would be a lot better when he was living in Stoneybrook. I even had a solution for the glove problem. After I mowed the lawn, I'd go to the sporting goods store in town and exchange it for a left-handed one. Then, if anyone asked me where I got my new glove, I'd say I finally had enough saved up for it. Everyone knew I was saving for one. For now it would be my secret that my dad — my very own dad — had given it to me.

I heard the chug-chug of our lawn mower and wondered if Watson was doing my job. He was. When he saw me he turned off the motor.

"Thanks for starting the lawn," I said. "I can finish it now."

"Okay." He wiped the sweat from his face with a handkerchief and smiled at me in the old familiar way. Nothing seemed unusual. He didn't question me, either. I wondered if he'd told Mom that I'd lied about baby-sitting.

As I took off my backpack, the baseball glove fell out. Watson picked it up, studied it for a second, and handed it back to me without saying anything. I quickly stuffed the glove in my pack again and restarted the lawn mower.

When I finished mowing, I went inside to wash up. Mom was making lunch. "Hi, honey," she said. "How did your job with the Barrett kids go?"

"Fine," I answered. "Nothing unusual."

When she accepted that, I knew Watson hadn't told on me.

That afternoon I told my mother I was going over to Mary Anne's house, which was true. I didn't tell her that first I was going to go to the sporting goods store to exchange my new glove.

As I walked into the store I was feeling pretty good. I'd have the baseball glove I needed and it would sort of be from my dad. I handed the new glove to the clerk. "I'd like to exchange this," I said. "It's a righty and I'm a lefty. The person who gave it to me didn't know."

The clerk looked the glove over, inside and out. "You sure he got it here?" he asked.

"I think so," I said.

"It's a Rawlings," he said. "And we carry those. But this glove wasn't bought here."

"Could you exchange it anyway?" I asked. "It's new and you carry Rawlings gloves."

"Look, Miss," he said. "It seems to me that

you're trying to pull a fast one on me."

My heart started pounding. Did he think I had shoplifted the glove and was now trying to exchange it? "I don't know what you're talking about," I said.

He looked me in the eye and seemed to be thinking something over. Finally he said, "I'll give you the benefit of the doubt. Maybe you don't know."

"Know what?" I asked.

"This glove has been personalized," he explained. "Something's printed inside." He held the glove open so I could see the print inside the heel. It read, "California Sportswriters Annual Awards Dinner."

"Your glove was a giveaway at some banquet," he continued. "Rawlings must have given them to all the journalists. You know, like a party favor. Is your friend a sportswriter?"

"Yes," I said. "He is."

The clerk handed me back the glove. I left the store in a hurry and rode to Mary Anne's. We went to her room so we could be private and I told her the whole story.

"It'd be different if he'd been honest with me," I told her. "I mean if he'd said, *'I got this glove at a banquet and I thought you could use it.'* But to say, *'It's a present for some of the birthdays*

I missed.' And then not to tell me it was a present someone gave him. I hate it. It's all wrong."

"Maybe it'll be different when he's living here," Mary Anne said. "Maybe you have to give him a second chance. He's probably not used to thinking about how other people feel."

"What really bothers me," I went on, "is that I can't tell him how he hurt me. I didn't even tell him I'm a lefty. To me if someone doesn't take the trouble to know you, that means they don't want to know you."

"I'm sorry he did that to you," Mary Anne said. She was crying.

"Come on, Mary Anne," I said. "Don't cry."

She wiped her eyes with a tissue. "I'm sorry."

"And don't be sorry," I said.

"Sorry I said I'm sorry."

That made us both smile.

"You were right," I told her. "Patrick is immature. He must have made a terrible husband for my mom."

"She had better luck with Watson," Mary Anne agreed. "He's pretty neat. You're lucky to have him for a stepfather."

"I guess," I said. Then I told her how Watson knew I had lied about baby-sitting that morning and hadn't told my mother.

I met Patrick for about an hour before my baby-sitting job the next evening. I still didn't tell him about the glove. I couldn't find the right words.

As it turned out, I never had a chance to tell him that his one and only daughter was a lefty. Because two days later Patrick Thomas skipped town and I haven't heard from him since. He didn't tell me he was leaving. He just didn't show up when I was supposed to meet him. He'd checked out of the hotel and was gone.

That's when I finally told my mother the whole story. She forgave me for all the lying I had done. "I wish you'd told me Patrick was here, though," she said. "I could have warned you a little about him."

"I don't think I would have listened to you," I said. "And you know what? I'm glad it happened. Now I really know what he's like."

I talked to Watson about what happened with my father, too. And I thanked him for keeping my secret when he caught me in a lie. He brushed off my thank you. "It was the thing to do in the situation," he said. "Besides, Kristy, you're a person I know and trust."

I thought, You're a person I know and trust, too. But all I said was "Well, thanks anyway."

Even though my mom and Watson were so nice to me, I felt pretty glum about all that had happened with Patrick. I'd built up a fantasy about what my life would be like if my real father lived in Stoneybrook. I also had a fantasy about what kind of person he was and how he felt about me. Now my fantasies had been replaced by reality.

When I came downstairs for dinner not long after Patrick skipped town, everyone in our family was already in the dining room. I pulled out my seat. A big box with a purple ribbon was on it. I looked up. Everyone was grinning at me. "What's this?" I asked.

"A present," said Charlie.

"It's from Daddy," Andrew added.

"It is from all of us," Karen corrected him. "Daddy just picked it out."

I looked around at my family. "Thank you," I said. "Thank you very much."

"Open it," said my mother.

I put the box on the table in front of me, untied the ribbon, pulled off the cover, and looked inside. "A baseball glove," I said. "Just what I needed."

Everyone laughed because I'd been saying I needed a new baseball glove for weeks. It was a glove for a lefty. I put it on. Then I hugged Watson and patted him on the shoulder with the mitt. "Thanks," I said.

A gift from a father I can trust.

"Use it in good health," he said. "And make a lot of catches."

"I will," I promised.

My real father may have disappointed me. But my stepfather would not. He knew me. He loved me. And he was there for me.

CHAPTER 15

I finished my autobiography late Sunday night and turned it in on Monday morning. When I had started my autobiography I thought I wouldn't have enough to write about. But by the time I finished it I'd thought of a dozen more stories about my life that I might have worked in. I could have written a five-hundred-page book on the first thirteen years of my life!

After I turned in my autobiography I found myself still thinking about it. At lunch on Monday I reminded Mary Anne and Claudia about the time we made the snowpeople and bought Mimi a scarf for her birthday.

"I wished I'd thought to write about that in my autobiography," said Claudia. "That was so much fun."

"I remember thinking how smart you were, Kristy," said Mary Anne. "Having a snow-person-building business was brilliant. You're the only person I know who could come up with an idea like that."

"Thanks," I said.

That night, at dinner, I reminded my brothers of the time I went to the soccer game and to see *Car Man* with them. We ended up telling our whole family the plot of that movie. Everyone was cracking up. Especially when Andrew tried to fit into Emily's toddler car so he could be Car Man. Charlie told him he had a better idea for being Car Man. He pinned one of Andrew's toy cars to the top of a baseball cap and put it on Andrew's head. "Wear this when you transform into Car Man," he told Andrew. "It fits you better than Emily's car."

Andrew *va-room-ed* and *honk-honk-ed* around the house with the plastic car bobbing on his head. Karen was the arch-villain, Fire Breath.

On Wednesday afternoon I had a Krushers practice game. To save time I told the kids to take the same sides they had taken at our last practice. By the third inning of the game I noticed that the two teams were not being very nice to one another. It reminded me of the Bluejays and the Robins at Camp Topnotch. I called a time-out and announced, "It's story hour."

The kids laughed at the idea of a story hour during softball practice, but they were happy to sit around me to hear a story. I noticed that they sat in two groups according to their practice teams. The bad feeling hung in the air between them.

"This story is about something that happened to a girl named Kristy," I began. "She went to a summer camp where you could play softball all day long." Then I told the Krushers the story of my experiences at Camp Topnotch. They laughed a lot at the pranks the Robins and Bluejays played on one another, but they were shocked when the coach quit.

"Are you going to quit because we're fighting?" Buddy Barrett asked.

"Should I?" I asked.

"No!" the Krushers shouted.

After that story, the rest of the practice game went very smoothly.

On Thursday I mowed our lawn after school. Watson came outside when I was about halfway through and trimmed the edges with the weed-eater. When we were putting the lawn mower and weed-eater back in the garage he asked me if I had gotten my autobiography back.

"We're getting them back tomorrow," I answered. "I wrote about you in mine. About when you surprised me with the new baseball glove."

"Hey, thanks," he said. He bowed. "I'm honored to be in your autobiography."

As we were going into the house I told him about the time our old dog Louie was sprayed by a skunk. And how Charlie, Sam, and I gave Louie a tomato juice bath. Watson thought that was pretty funny. Then he told me that a light spray of clear vinegar is a much better antidote for skunk smell. "Put clear vinegar in a spray bottle and spray the animal," he said, "but be careful not to get any in his eyes. And you don't have to rinse the vinegar off."

"Thanks," I told Watson. "I hope I never have to use your advice for Shannon." Just then I thought I saw a skunk running under a bush. We ran into the house, laughing.

But the next morning during English class I wasn't laughing. I was nervous about the grade I would get on my autobiography. I'd worked hard on it and I thought it was pretty good. But what if Mrs. Simon didn't agree with me? Maybe I had written too much about softball. Maybe she wouldn't understand why I had lied to my wonderful mother to protect my not-so-wonderful father. Would she take off points if she disapproved of me? I crossed my fingers under my desk and waited as Mrs. Simon called my classmates one by one to collect their graded autobiographies from her desk.

Finally, she called my name. I carried *Thirteen Years in the Life of Kristin Amanda Thomas* back to my desk, opened the front cover, and read:

Mrs. Simon
—◊◊—

B⁺ Very good work, Kristy. You related incidents from your life with insight and humor.

I didn't realize you were so accomplished at athletics and business. You run the Baby-sitters Club _and_ a softball team for younger children. I'm impressed.

Keep up the good work in English, too.

M.S.

L. GODWIN

Ann M. Martin

About the Author

ANN MATTHEWS MARTIN was born on August 12, 1955. She grew up in Princeton, NJ, with her parents and her younger sister, Jane.

Although Ann used to be a teacher and then an editor of children's books, she's now a full-time writer. She gets the ideas for her books from many different places. Some are based on personal experiences. Others are based on childhood memories and feelings. Many are written about contemporary problems or events.

All of Ann's characters, even the members of the Baby-sitters Club, are made up. (So is Stoneybrook.) But many of her characters are based on real people. Sometimes Ann names her characters after people she knows, other times she chooses names she likes.

In addition to the Baby-sitters Club books, Ann Martin has written many other books for children. Her favorite is *Ten Kids, No Pets* because she loves big families and she loves animals. Her favorite Baby-sitters Club book is *Kristy's Big Day*. (By the way, Kristy is her favorite baby-sitter!)

Ann M. Martin now lives in New York with her cats, Gussie and Woody. Her hobbies are reading, sewing, and needlework — especially making clothes for children.

Read all the books
about **Kristy**
in the Baby-sitters Club series
by Ann M. Martin

\# 1 *Kristy's Great Idea*
Kristy's great idea is to start *The Baby-sitters Club*!

\# 6 *Kristy's Big Day*
Kristy's a baby-sitter — and a bridesmaid, too!

\# 11 *Kristy and the Snobs*
The kids in Kristy's new neighborhood are
S-N-O-B-S!

\# 20 *Kristy and the Walking Disaster*
Can Kristy's Krushers beat Bart's Bashers?

\# 24 *Kristy and the Mother's Day Surprise*
Emily Michelle is the big surprise!

\# 32 *Kristy and the Secret of Susan*
Even Kristy can't learn all of Susan's secrets.

\# 38 *Kristy's Mystery Admirer*
Someone is sending Kristy *love notes*!

\# 45 *Kristy and the Baby Parade*
Will the Baby-sitters' float take first prize in the
Stoneybrook Baby Parade?

\# 53 *Kristy for President*
Can Kristy run the BSC and the whole eighth
grade?

\# 62 *Kristy and the Worst Kid Ever*
Need a baby-sitter for Lou? Don't call the Baby-
sitters Club!

\# 74 *Kristy and the Copycat*
Kristy's done something bad — something she'd
never want Karen to copy.

81 *Kristy and Mr. Mom*
Kristy's stepfather Watson has a new job!

89 *Kristy and the Dirty Diapers*
Will Kristy lose the Krushers when they change
their name to the Diapers?

95 *Kristy + Bart = ?*
Are Kristy and Bart more than just friends?

#100 *Kristy's Worst Idea*
Is this the end of the BSC?

Mysteries:

4 *Kristy and the Missing Child*
Kristy organizes a search party to help the police
find a missing child.

9 *Kristy and the Haunted Mansion*
Kristy and the Krashers are spending the night
in a spooky old house!

15 *Kristy and the Vampires*
A vampire movie is being shot in Stoneybrook.
Can Kristy and the BSC find out who's out to get
the star?

19 *Kristy and the Missing Fortune*
It could all be Kristy's — if she and the BSC crack
the case.

25 *Kristy and the Middle School Vandal*
Cary Retlin is up to his old tricks — and Kristy
has to stop him!

Portrait Collection:

Kristy's Book
The official autobiography of Kristin Amanda
Thomas.

How well do YOU know your BSC trivia?

THE BABY-SITTERS CLUB®

Summer Sweeps

HEY FANS! *BSC Book #100 is coming soon—* can you believe it?—and we're celebrating its arrival with an awesome trivia sweepstakes all summer long!

✶✶✶✶✶✶✶✶✶✶

Enter now to win a part in a future BSC book *plus* more than 100 other sweepstakes prizes!

Enter To Win 100+ Prizes

GRAND PRIZE:
✶ You will be featured in a future BSC story
✶ A complete wardrobe from LA Gear including an extralarge duffle bag, sweatshirt, t-shirt, baseball cap, shoes, water bottle, and leather CD carrying case
✶ *The BSC The Movie* video
✶ *The BSC The Movie* sound track
✶ BSC t-Shirt
✶ *The Complete Guide to The BSC*—autographed by Ann M. Martin

10 FIRST PRIZES:
✶ BSC t-Shirt
✶ *The Complete Guide to The BSC*—autographed by Ann M. Martin

100 RUNNERS-UP:
✶ BSC t-Shirt

It's easy! Just answer the ten questions on the back of this sheet, fill-in your name and address, and send back to us!

SCSC296

MORE ▶

How well do YOU know your BSC trivia?

THE BABY-SITTERS CLUB®
Summer Sweeps

The Questions:

✻1. The BSC meets on these days: _____, _____, and _____.

✻2. What day of the week is dues day? _____.

✻3. What is the name of the box (with games) that Kristy invented for charges? ___ ___.

✻4. BSC meetings begin at: _____

✻5. Whose bedroom are BSC meetings held in? _____ _____.

✻6. Which member sits in the director's chair at club meetings? _____ _____.

✻7. Who is originally from New York City? _____ _____

✻8. How many brothers and sisters does Mallory have? _____.

✻9. Which two members are only eleven years old? _____ and _____.

✻10. Friends. Members of the BSC. What else do Mary Anne and Dawn have in common? _____.

✻✻✻✻✻✻✻✻✻✻

Enter me in The BSC Summer Sweeps!
I am including the answers to the 10 questions.

Name_____ Birthdate___ ___ ___
      First   Last   m / d / y

Street_____

City_____ State_____ Zip Code_____

(check boxes section please)
Tell Us Where You Got This Book!

__ Bookstore   __ Book Club   __ Book Fair

__ Price Club   __ Other _____

THE BABY-SITTERS CLUB®

The best friends you'll ever have!

Collect 'em all!

by Ann M. Martin

❑ MG43388-1	#1	Kristy's Great Idea	$3.50
❑ MG43387-3	#10	Logan Likes Mary Anne!	$3.99
❑ MG43717-8	#15	Little Miss Stoneybrook...and Dawn	$3.50
❑ MG43722-4	#20	Kristy and the Walking Disaster	$3.50
❑ MG43347-4	#25	Mary Anne and the Search for Tigger	$3.50
❑ MG42498-X	#30	Mary Anne and the Great Romance	$3.50
❑ MG42508-0	#35	Stacey and the Mystery of Stoneybrook	$3.50
❑ MG44082-9	#40	Claudia and the Middle School Mystery	$3.25
❑ MG43574-4	#45	Kristy and the Baby Parade	$3.50
❑ MG44969-9	#50	Dawn's Big Date	$3.50
❑ MG44968-0	#51	Stacey's Ex-Best Friend	$3.50
❑ MG44966-4	#52	Mary Anne + 2 Many Babies	$3.50
❑ MG44967-2	#53	Kristy for President	$3.25
❑ MG44965-6	#54	Mallory and the Dream Horse	$3.25
❑ MG44964-8	#55	Jessi's Gold Medal	$3.25
❑ MG45657-1	#56	Keep Out, Claudia!	$3.50
❑ MG45658-X	#57	Dawn Saves the Planet	$3.50
❑ MG45659-8	#58	Stacey's Choice	$3.50
❑ MG45660-1	#59	Mallory Hates Boys (and Gym)	$3.50
❑ MG45662-8	#60	Mary Anne's Makeover	$3.50
❑ MG45663-6	#61	Jessi and the Awful Secret	$3.50
❑ MG45664-4	#62	Kristy and the Worst Kid Ever	$3.50
❑ MG45665-2	#63	Claudia's Special Friend	$3.50
❑ MG45666-0	#64	Dawn's Family Feud	$3.50
❑ MG45667-9	#65	Stacey's Big Crush	$3.50
❑ MG47004-3	#66	Maid Mary Anne	$3.50
❑ MG47005-1	#67	Dawn's Big Move	$3.50
❑ MG47006-X	#68	Jessi and the Bad Baby-sitter	$3.50
❑ MG47007-8	#69	Get Well Soon, Mallory!	$3.50
❑ MG47008-6	#70	Stacey and the Cheerleaders	$3.50
❑ MG47009-4	#71	Claudia and the Perfect Boy	$3.50
❑ MG47010-8	#72	Dawn and the We Love Kids Club	$3.50
❑ MG47011-6	#73	Mary Anne and Miss Priss	$3.50
❑ MG47012-4	#74	Kristy and the Copycat	$3.50
❑ MG47013-2	#75	Jessi's Horrible Prank	$3.50
❑ MG47014-0	#76	Stacey's Lie	$3.50
❑ MG48221-1	#77	Dawn and Whitney, Friends Forever	$3.50
❑ MG48222-X	#78	Claudia and Crazy Peaches	$3.50

More titles... ▸

The Baby-sitters Club titles continued...

❑ MG48223-8	#79	**Mary Anne Breaks the Rules**	$3.50
❑ MG48224-6	#80	**Mallory Pike, #1 Fan**	$3.50
❑ MG48225-4	#81	**Kristy and Mr. Mom**	$3.50
❑ MG48226-2	#82	**Jessi and the Troublemaker**	$3.50
❑ MG48235-1	#83	**Stacey vs. the BSC**	$3.50
❑ MG48228-9	#84	**Dawn and the School Spirit War**	$3.50
❑ MG48236-X	#85	**Claudi Kishli, Live from WSTO**	$3.50
❑ MG48227-0	#86	**Mary Anne and Camp BSC**	$3.50
❑ MG48237-8	#87	**Stacey and the Bad Girls**	$3.50
❑ MG22872-2	#88	**Farewell, Dawn**	$3.50
❑ MG22873-0	#89	**Kristy and the Dirty Diapers**	$3.50
❑ MG22874-9	#90	**Welcome to the BSC, Abby**	$3.50
❑ MG22875-1	#91	**Claudia and the First Thanksgiving**	$3.50
❑ MG22876-5	#92	**Mallory's Christmas Wish**	$3.50
❑ MG22877-3	#93	**Mary Anne and the Memory Garden**	$3.99
❑ MG22878-1	#94	**Stacey McGill, Super Sitter**	$3.99
❑ MG22879-X	#95	**Kristy + Bart = ?**	$3.99
❑ MG22880-3	#96	**Abby's Lucky Thirteen**	$3.99
❑ MG22881-1	#97	**Claudia and the World's Cutest Baby**	$3.99
❑ MG22882-X	#98	**Dawn and Too Many Baby-sitters**	$3.99
❑ MG69205-4	#99	**Stacey's Broken Heart**	$3.99
❑ MG45575-3		**Logan's Story Special Edition Readers' Request**	$3.25
❑ MG47118-X		**Logan Bruno, Boy Baby-sitter**	
		Special Edition Readers' Request	$3.50
❑ MG47756-0		**Shannon's Story Special Edition**	$3.50
❑ MG47686-6		**The Baby-sitters Club Guide to Baby-sitting**	$3.25
❑ MG47314-X		**The Baby-sitters Club Trivia and Puzzle Fun Book**	$2.50
❑ MG48400-1		**BSC Portrait Collection: Claudia's Book**	$3.50
❑ MG22864-1		**BSC Portrait Collection: Dawn's Book**	$3.50
❑ MG22865-X		**BSC Portrait Collection: Mary Anne's Book**	$3.99
❑ MG48399-4		**BSC Portrait Collection: Stacey's Book**	$3.50
❑ MG47151-1		**The Baby-sitters Club Chain Letter**	$14.95
❑ MG48295-5		**The Baby-sitters Club Secret Santa**	$14.95
❑ MG45074-3		**The Baby-sitters Club Notebook**	$2.50
❑ MG44783-1		**The Baby-sitters Club Postcard Book**	$4.95

Available wherever you buy books...or use this order form.
Scholastic Inc., P.O. Box 7502, 2931 E. McCarty Street, Jefferson City, MO 65102

Please send me the books I have checked above. I am enclosing $_____
(please add $2.00 to cover shipping and handling). Send check or money order—
no cash or C.O.D.s please.

Name_____ Birthdate_____

Address _____

City_____ State/Zip _____

BSC296

THE BABY-SITTERS CLUB®

by Ann M. Martin

Collect and read these exciting BSC Super Specials, Mysteries, and Super Mysteries along with your favorite Baby-sitters Club books!

BSC Super Specials

❑ BBK44240-6	Baby-sitters on Board! Super Special #1	$3.95
❑ BBK44239-2	Baby-sitters' Summer Vacation Super Special #2	$3.95
❑ BBK43973-1	Baby-sitters' Winter Vacation Super Special #3	$3.95
❑ BBK42493-9	Baby-sitters' Island Adventure Super Special #4	$3.95
❑ BBK43575-2	California Girls! Super Special #5	$3.95
❑ BBK43576-0	New York, New York! Super Special #6	$3.95
❑ BBK44963-X	Snowbound! Super Special #7	$3.95
❑ BBK44962-X	Baby-sitters at Shadow Lake Super Special #8	$3.95
❑ BBK45661-X	Starring The Baby-sitters Club! Super Special #9	$3.95
❑ BBK45674-1	Sea City, Here We Come! Super Special #10	$3.95
❑ BBK47015-9	The Baby-sitters Remember Super Special #11	$3.95
❑ BBK48308-0	Here Come the Bridesmaids! Super Special #12	$3.95

BSC Mysteries

❑ BAI44084-5	#1	Stacey and the Missing Ring	$3.50
❑ BAI44085-3	#2	Beware Dawn!	$3.50
❑ BAI44799-8	#3	Mallory and the Ghost Cat	$3.50
❑ BAI44800-5	#4	Kristy and the Missing Child	$3.50
❑ BAI44801-3	#5	Mary Anne and the Secret in the Attic	$3.50
❑ BAI44961-3	#6	The Mystery at Claudia's House	$3.50
❑ BAI44960-5	#7	Dawn and the Disappearing Dogs	$3.50
❑ BAI44959-1	#8	Jessi and the Jewel Thieves	$3.50
❑ BAI44958-3	#9	Kristy and the Haunted Mansion	$3.50

More titles ➡

The Baby-sitters Club books continued...